ADVANCED PRAISE FOR LOVE WINS: NIKKI'S TALE

"It's not every day that an author not only draws you in with their words, but also their emotional connection to the story all at once. I can assure you that there will be moments placing you into the story as if you are remembering the past as well. You are going to love the experience."

~ Michael H.

From the very first page, Love Wins had me locked in since it took me back to MY teenage years! The nostalgia was real, and the characters were so relatable!! Life is not a game nor a fairy tale, and this book reminds us that life is always about the long game, not the short fix. I encourage everyone to take the ride with Nikki - it's worth the trip.

~Dione R.

Love Wins

Love Wins
NIKKI'S TALE
LaDina Strawder

Love Wins: Nikki's Tale

ISBN: 979-8-218-19445-1

Published by: R.I.C.E. Publishing, LLC.
Printed in the United States of America
Edited By: Dione Rawlings, Yulanda Johnson, and Penda James

Internal Layout and Design: InSCRIBEd Inspiration, LLC.
Cover Art: Ikenna N. Chineme Art
Cover Design: Soleil Branding Essentials

DEDICATION

Lorraine, this book is published because of you. Your enthusiasm for my draft made me want to write more. Your questioning of when I would write the sequel encouraged me to give you what you were looking for. I hope I made you proud, sis. While I had hoped we'd share this moment together physically, I know you are in heaven rooting for me still.

Love, THANK YOU. Thank you for your transparency, patience, kindness, honesty, charm, your word being your bond, and energy. Thank you for helping unearth a femininity in me I never thought I had. Showing me how I would want a man to actually care for me (show me love) and stay out of my head-stop imagining the worst when it hasn't even happened. For this book, I release my imagination but not for the worst, because of you *wink* – Nikki

Love Wins

CONTENTS

Introduction: Nikki's Tale ix
1992 1
Senior Year: 1994 7
Prom 11
Prom Day 19
Camille Carter 31
The Get Down 41
Love 57
Sometimes You Want What You Want 73
Essex 81
Nicole 89
The Straw That Ended It All 95
Happy Endings 109
Five Years Later 117

Introduction: Nikki's Tale

You never realize you are living in survival mode until you are sitting in it. When that moment arrives, it will require you to unpack every toxic bag you have ever carried. Whether your mode of awareness and release is therapy, confiding in friends, a deliverance service, or just a good shedding through journaling, the shit is not easy, believe me.

The character, Nicole in this book is not a real person. She does, however, have real life experiences. I write this book for the Nicole's in my life who have come to me for advice, support or counseling. Nicole is all of us when we don't heal. We go through the stages of loss like a hamster on a wheel, wondering, "Will I ever make it out of this alive and healed?"

Let's imagine that Nicole and I are talking. She is recalling her trauma as if she had just experienced it. She described her 8-year-old self vividly to me. I could see her in her room being cared for by her older cousin. I could imagine her mom having fun while out with friends; something she rarely did.

The air in Nicole's room was humid with a light breeze from the cracked window to keep her from as she said, "sweating to death." I know that she had just fallen asleep after watching *Goonies* for the third time that day, it was her favorite movie. I can see her face as she retells me the scene when Chunk throws the Baby Ruth at Sloth. I know that Nicole needed to connect with a happier time before she delved into unpacking her trauma.

I can imagine Nicole recollecting that she was awakened by her seventeen-year-old cousin rubbing on her "cooch" and feeling a poke in her stomach because his dick was erect. She didn't know what it was then, but she soon found out.

I can see Nicole trying to push his hand away and realizing that he had become more forceful. She remembers him telling her, "Stop moving, I won't hurt you."

She sighed, "I guess he believed that would make me at ease. It didn't." For Nicole, his disgusting act had heavy repercussions on her psyche and future relationships.

I feel for Nicole as she begins to cry for her eight-year-old self during our session. "I couldn't protect my eight-year-old self." Nicole mourns because she could not stop someone, she and her mother trusted from taking her innocence, and virginity." I trusted him and he was supposed to care for me."

Nicole explained that her compounded grief from the situation grew heavier when she told her mother the next day. "After he left, I told her. She scolded me and told me to stop lying on my cousin."

I could relate to Nicole when she stated that her mother told her to not bring it up anymore. He got to babysit her even after the incident.

I asked Nicole, "Did you tell anyone else?"

Nicole indicated that she had not told her father because he was already out of the home and didn't want him to be out of her life, if he found out. "I saw how he was about me with boys on the street he lived on when I would visit him." She cried and said, "I held on to this secret as if it had never happened."

Many of us are like Nicole Bentley. We question our whole existence because of the trauma we have experienced. We wonder if love is a real thing.

For Nicole a divine encounter changed her life. The day that Nicole met DeVaughn Lovely or "Love," Nicole knew that she wanted more of what she felt. For the love she experienced, Nicole was willing to risk it all.

Nicole had experienced enough sadness in life, and "Love" seemed to remedy her pain. She would soon realize that Love was not an ordinary man; he was the epitome of love.

1992

"Giiirl! I can't wait to get to school today!" I said as I looked into my vanity while inserting my bamboo earrings into my ears. I adjusted the painting I had just painted on my wall; it was the first of many I'd make. My mom said I had a real gift for the arts.

"Why?" my friend Camille asked.

I turned and gave her that "Stop playing, you know" look. And she did; I could tell by her smile.

"So you can see Looove," Camille said.

My face lit up just hearing his name.

Love was his street name, short for his last name because of his way with the ladies. There was an interest in him that I never allowed going any further than a kiss.

His government name was DeVaughn Lovely. I loved to call him by his government name when we were alone, which wasn't often. It was sexy to me. Calling him DeVaughn made a deeper, more intimate connection to show him I see him, not just the street guy everyone else saw him as. I hoped he noticed.

"You know it!" I high-fived Camille, swung my hips, and snapped my fingers to "Don't Walk Away" by Jade on the radio.

When I thought back, 1992-1993 were my favorite years. Love and I were associates, but I had the biggest crush on him, and he wasn't even aware. We were flirty, but nothing transpired from it.

Camille interrupted my daydreaming and asked, "Nikki, why don't you just say something to him? You already know how he feels about you. You ain't losing nothing by saying you're interested."

I applied my eyeliner as Mary J's "What's the 411" began to play through the speakers. "I don't want to look like no ho," I told her.

We all knew how Love and his crew got down, running through triflin' ass chicks. I was *not* gonna be among those casualties. I did my dirt; I was just particular with whom I did it with.

"Ho? Sis, he knows how you get down… we ain't about that ho life," Camille reminded me.

"Jason would kill me if he knew I was trying to get with Love," I told Camille.

"Jason just be talking shit, he ain't…" Camille interrupted me.

"Jason ain't talking. He all about knocking a nigga out about his big little cuz, and he told me and Love what he would do if he found out, and I believe him," I cut Camille off sternly.

"How'd he even know ya'll like each other? I never took Jason as the crazy type," Camille added.

"Welcome to my world! He may be younger than me and not in my circle all the time, but he's hot-headed and violent when it comes to his cousin. All I can do is respect that," I responded.

My cousin Jason (my mother's brother Earl's son), Wink as we called him cause of his lashes that just brought out his hazel eyes, and I were like siblings. He was only a month and a couple of days younger than me, but still, he saw himself as the big cousin, and I let him. Jason was so overprotective of me. It was a bit annoying at times, but when a nigga I didn't like wanted to rap to me, I would tell Jason, and that would be the end of it. He had become more overprotective after knowing someone in the family molested me; I never told him who it was because he would've killed him. Literally, he was that crazy.

I finished brushing my hair down from my wrap into my infamous silky bob. I double-checked myself in the mirror, ensuring my booty sat out how I liked and blew myself a kiss.

"You are so damn conceited," Camille said, shaking her head.

"It's not conceit, my dear. It's confidence," I told her. "Self-love. Come on before we're late for school." I dragged her out of my room so we didn't miss our 7:30 a.m. PAT bus to school.

We stepped off the bus, half a block from the school, and who did we see walking toward us? Yup, it was Love and his crew.

"Here we go," Camille said. "Sis, here's your chance. He's looking right at you."

I looked up, and Love was looking into my soul with his sexy brown eyes, all while continuing his conversation with his crew. He motioned with his index finger for me to come over to where they were. I tried to ignore him and almost walked into a pole until Camille jerked my arm to get my attention. Embarrassed, I started speed walking into school; I didn't even look back to see Love's expression.

Camille made me feel bad for not going over to him. "See, you would have missed the pole if you had just gone over there."

"I told you, I ain't trying to look like I'm chasing a nigga. They chase me." I winked at her.

We laughed, high-fived one another and said in unison, "Sho ya right!"

I told Camille, "If I see him in the hallway, I'll say hi. Gotta have the thrill of the chase. But if I do, you have to call that dude you met at Sherry's party."

"That's a start", she replied as she closed her locker door. "What, dude? I know you ain't talking about Joel?"

"Is that his name?!" With a sheepish smile, Camille smacked my forearm and swore she was not into him.

"Y'all was slow winding like he can get it," I said, giving her that "I don't believe that shit at all" look.

"Joel is just my friend and a great dance partner," Camille retorted.

"You know about the guys that can dance like that?" I began to gyrate my hips, and Camille was now blushing and pushing me to stop. I almost slammed into the locker, walking down the hall. "I'm just saying, sis, see what's up… I think he likes you anyway."

"Girl, he got a baby on the way," Camille blurted out.

That stopped my gyrating, and I looked at her in disbelief. "For real?!"

"Hell yeah, he told me last night when he walked me home."

I could hear the disappointment in her voice, but being the person I was, I said some stupid shit to cheer her up. "Sis, you just dodged a motherfucking bullet."

She gave me that "thanks, but no thanks, sis" smile.

I asked, "Too soon?"

"Yeah."

"My bad… I can't lie. I liked him."

We sat in silence until I couldn't take it anymore. A throwback came on as we entered the cafeteria, "It Takes Two" by Rob Base and DJ EZ Rock. For the moment, Joel was a non-factor. We busted a dance move in the lunch line.

Camille and I were always making up dance steps. We really should've gone professional with it, but I digress.

Senior Year: 1994

High school was ending, and Camille and I were trying to decide who to go to the prom with. We both knew we didn't want anyone that couldn't dance. Besides, we had to start early because we wanted our dresses made, and these dressmakers were booked by January. Not only that, but we also had to prepare for Senior pics; I had my appointment scheduled already. As we sat in my room, we discussed some of our plans.

"Sis, did you schedule your Senior pic yet?" I asked Camille.

"Yes, but I couldn't get in 'til September 17th."

"Where?" I asked.

"Strem-Varden, downtown"

"Me too! I'm going on the same day! We can go together!" I was excited that my best friend and I could do our Senior pics together.

She asked, "Did you set your hair appointment?"

"Nope, not yet."

"Now, you know our hair has to be on point for these pics. Call now so you can get in," she admonished me.

"All right."

I picked up the phone to call Precious Styles. "Hi, Precious, this is Nikki. I'm calling to schedule with you for next Friday. Please, call me to confirm." I turned to Camille and said, "Done," as I hung up.

"You sound like a white girl talking on that phone." Camille laughed.

"Don't be a hater, sis." I threw the pillow at her as I giggled, knowing I sounded just like a white girl.

"So, did you ever call the dude from the college tour? What was his name?" Camille asked.

"Girl, no!" I exclaimed. "His kissing game was weak as hell. Cousin Sandy always said, 'If they can't kiss or dance, they can't fuck.' I found that shit to be true."

We both laughed.

"So, who's your date to the prom then?" she asked, assuming I had no potential options.

"Girl, you know how I roll." I pulled out my black book. "These niggas ain't the only ones with prospects."

As a Senior, I had become a bit more sexually active and was really out to play these niggas. If they thought they had me, I was already scheming on how I would beat them for their dough. I never dated a guy who had no money; I made certain of that.

"What about Leslie, Tee, Hank, Bull… nah, David?!" I said with expectant hope that he would say yes for so many reasons.

"Sis, you fittin' to act up!" Camille laughed at the thought of knowing how I got down. "He's perfect. I hope he says yes."

"Who are you thinking of asking?" I returned the question.

"Well, Joel and I have been talking again." She hesitated. "So…"

"What?!" I asked curiously. "What's the 'so' for?"

"His baby's mom. She out here clowning and threatening us if we go to prom together," Camille said with concern in her voice. "He says he understands if I want to take someone else."

"So, who you taking?" I said, snapping my neck, indicating she needed to do just that and find someone else. "What about that dude Mike?"

"Mike, from Larimer?"

"Yeah, he ain't a bad look with his chocolate, fine ass," I said, recalling his short chocolate stature, with fine black hair he kept neatly braided in cornrows.

"He is fine, but he's too short, and he smokes. I don't know."

Camille wasn't really feeling the suggestion. She had stopped dating him because she had to bend to kiss him, and his breath smelled like cigarettes. That wasn't her preference.

"Okay, what about…" Camille stopped me as if she had an epiphany. "I got it! Lamar!" she let out.

"Girl, yes! Now that's the one!"

We both shook our heads in agreement cause the boy was *fiiine*.

"Yes! Tall?" I said.

"Check!" Camille responded.

"Chocolate?"

"Check!"

"Can kiss?"

"Check. Check!"

"Can dance?"

"Check. Check. Check!"

We fell back on my bed in laughter. Knocking my "King/Queen" painting right onto our heads. I was relieved it didn't rip.

"I'll call him tonight; I know he works until seven this evening," she reported.

"I know he will say yes, 'cause he loooves some Camille, so…" I tickled her arm, knowing her assignment was easy.

Prom

Senior year had gone by so quickly, and I anticipated the prom and graduation to be memorable. David did say yes to my prom invitation. Lamar said yes to Camille. We were so excited. We planned to have a ball!

I jumped as I closed my locker from putting my trig book back from class. Love was posted up behind it and scared the shit out of me. He just stared at me without even speaking. It was weird and made me want to disappear. So I just said hello with an attitude.

He calmly but passionately asked, "You really going to prom with some other nigga?"

"Uhm, I'm not following," I said confusedly.

"Nikki, you really going with this dude?" he repeated.

Yeah, Love, I'm really going with David. I don't understand what the problem is."

"The problem is you should be going with me and not this nigga." he said as if I had declined his proposal for him to take me.

"Love, you never asked me. I never knew you wanted to go to prom with me," I continued. "Besides, we hardly ever talk. One kiss, and you think I can read your mind?"

I pressed against my locker to make sure it

was shut. He walked up to me, towering over me, grabbed my face with his hands, and kissed me. Now I was discombobulated because this boy kissed me in front of everyone. He told me to save a dance for him and walked away. That was some smooth-ass shit, I tell you.

Oh yeah, I didn't tell ya'll. Love and I met up… nothing serious two months before asking David to the prom. My homegirls and I were walking down the block his house was on, and he happened to be, as usual, with his crew. One of his homeboys tapped him and nodded in our direction. He and his crew walked up to us to block us from walking any further.

His homeboy Nelson said, "You know y'all can't come any further unless ya girl." He nodded in my direction. "Gives this man here a kiss." He placed his hand on Love's shoulder like he was making us an offer I couldn't refuse.

My homegirls were some of the shadiest heifers I could have ever been friends with, but I still loved them. These chicks pushed me into Love as if to say, "Take one for the team. You know you want to anyway."

Love grabbed me by the waist and bent to lay one wet, tongue-infused kiss on me… all I tasted was the cinnamon Big Red gum he had been chewing. Man, not that I'd never been kissed, but damn, not like that and now I had to play it cool so as not to draw attention that a playa was down. Camille and the crew saw my eyes, immediately grabbed me, and began walking away.

I didn't look back, but the ladies told me Love had a big-ass cheese on his face, like he had bagged me. I could hear Nelson yelling for us to come back, but we kept walking and fast. I took one for the team, and at that moment, my heart took a deeper liking to Love.

All the way to our block, all they kept asking was, "How was it? Did his breath stink? Can he kiss?"

All I said was, "I won't kiss and tell, but like Cousin Sandy said, 'If he can kiss…'"

Camille and I said in unison, "He can fuck."

The ladies fell out laughing.

I added, "Don't y'all try and test him, 'cause he's mine." Yeah, I tagged him as mine and didn't tell him. He didn't need to know how I really felt at the time. Everyone in his and my crew and I could tell the feelings were mutual; it was only a matter of time.

I honestly couldn't tell Love I liked him because of his lifestyle. Love was what one would call a "dope boy." He was part of a group that fought, stole cars, sold drugs and whatnot—not activities I wanted to be associated with. He and his boys were cool when it came to my homegirls and me, but we vowed not to be caught up by these guys because they were out in these streets. They had lost two of their boys (our classmates) the summer before we graduated. All we knew was we didn't want to be casualties in the war, so we "entertained" from a distance.

After Love's and my second kiss at my locker, all I could taste was that damn Big Red, like, "Can't he chew something else?" Slightly embarrassed others had seen our interaction, I quietly walked downstairs to my last class of the day, study hall, where I had 45 minutes to think about what just went down. I started writing in my journal; my therapist suggested I write to process my feelings, so I did.

"I can't believe Love would be that bold to kiss me in front of everyone! I was so not expecting that. Other than the one kiss, it's not like he has asked me out or told me himself that he liked me. We just flirted, so how was I to know how he felt? I'm not a fucking mind reader… ugh. Now I have these feelings, and I don't know where to start to figure out what to do next. My homegirls feel I should tell him how I feel and just put it out there, but the way

he is all in these females' faces gives me a clear indication I'm not the only one. I don't like that. I'm too possessive and jealous when it comes to dating to have some nigga having me looking crazy because he got me on rotation, and I don't even know it. Nah, I'm good. But Love just has a vibe I cannot fucking shake, I want to, but he draws me in like a snake being charmed by a charmer. He is a charmer, that's for certain. If being addicted feels like this, I see why people re-up and forget their priorities. The shit's no joke.

I mean, he didn't ask me not to go with David. I assumed he just couldn't believe I didn't ask him. One kiss with casual flirtation doesn't mean we would attend prom. See, this is the bull I don't want to have to deal with, figuring out what's on a man's mind… no thanks. I'll have a lot to unpack in therapy tonight 'cause I can't."

I'd soon find that being attentive or a mind reader was something I would find myself doing way too often in my adult relationships. I'd also discover that type of relationship was toxic and messed with your mental health—stay clear. Communication in a relationship should be clear and consistent and allow you to ask questions without feeling as if you are being dismissed, gaslit or overdramatic.

Just telling you some things I would say to

my younger self.

Days Before the Prom

"Well, ain't this a motherfucking bitch!"

I was on my bed crying to Camille as I told her that David had broken his ankle at his basketball game and couldn't escort me to the prom. "This messed up my whole plan... ugh!" I knew it was out of my control, but everything I planned for prom would have been amazing.

Camille said in such a best-friend kind of way, "Sis, you got options. Don't cry when you have options." She added with suspense in her voice, "I hear Love is still looking for a date!"

"I'm not asking him!" I instantly replied.

"OK, don't...."

That heffa hung up on me. The next thing I knew, my phone rang.

"Chick, why you hang up?!" I asked with irritation in my voice.

The person on the other end responded, "Hey, Nikki."

I asked in shock and disbelief, "DeVaughn?"

"Yeah, what's good with you?" he asked.

"I'm not," I said, trying to hold back tears.

"I heard, but you can still go. You'll just go with me," Love reassured me.

"Is that an invitation to take me to the prom?" I was irritated by his whack-ass proposal.

"Yeah?" he confusingly responded.

"Uhm, naw, nigga," I replied.

"Wait, what I miss? You need a date for the prom, and I'm saying I'll take you. What's the problem, babe?" Love asked.

"You can at least ask *properly!* I don't know what kind of females you used to, but you ain't gonna just tell me what I'm going to do. You can ask," I demanded.

With a chuckle and his chill-ass ways, he said, "All right, my dearest Nikki, would you allow me to take you to the prom, your highness?"

I laughed. "You're such a smart ass, but, yes, I'll go with you. But tell all ya other broads 'cause I don't want to beat a bitch up in my badass dress, m'kay?"

He chuckled. "So, what color are we wearing? I need to go get something like today since we only have two weeks."

"Purple. I'll show you a picture of my dress tomorrow," I said.

"Cool, I'll see you tomorrow then, beautiful," he said in his most charming tone.

"Cool," I said with my face in full blush mode.

"Bye."

I stopped him before he hung up, "DeVaughn!"

"Yeah?"

"Thanks… bye."

"You can thank me later, babe. Bye."

I pressed end on that big ass portable house phone (why were those things so damn big?!). I fell into bed in relief and excitement. I would be going to the prom with DeVaughn Lovely! A win for him; a bigger win for me. God must've been up to something even then.

Prom Day

I woke to my alarm, singing Brandy's "Best Friend." I stretched, hopped out the bed and went into the bathroom to get my day started.

My agenda was set; I had to go to Venetian to get my nails and toes done and then on to my hair appointment. I was too geeked! My stylist and I tested my hairstyle prior to today, so I knew I would be looking fly as hell. My girl Khi was coming past later to do my makeup. When I say she was the bomb… she was a bomb-ass makeup artist. Good thing I had my license and my mom let me use her car; she said she'd have her coworker drop her off.

I stepped out of the house to the smell of spring, almost summer. The sky was fair, with the sun aggressively trying to peek through. I locked the door and began walking to my mom's Saturn. I loved that car. My girls and I went everywhere in that thing, parties, pull-ups, creeps, you name it (laughing on the inside about our dirt)!

I felt a tap on my shoulder, and I froze up. I turned, and it was Love.

"Damn, man. What is wrong with you, DeVaughn?!" I said as I exhaled.

He was cracking up.

"You're an asshole. You scared the life out of me."

"Where you off to early in the morning?"

"I have a lot to do before tonight. Sorry I can't throw a suit on and go like you," I said sarcastically. I added, "I can't wait to see you in your suit." I stroked his chest and smiled, just imagining Love in a suit.

"I can't wait to see you tonight either," he said with his sheepish grin.

"Bye, DeVaughn," I said with a sigh as I looked at him and opened the car door.

"Oh, let me get that for you," he said as if he had forgotten his manners.

"Thank you, DeVaughn." I winked and slid into the driver's seat. I added, "Where are you going so early in the morning?"

"Oh, now you worried about where I'm going? My feelings are hurt."

"Man, where you headed?" I giggled as I asked.

"Barbershop." He winked.

"Good, 'cause, man, you wolfing!" I teased.

"You know I stay fresh to death, don't even try it," he said, smiling.

"I know, I know… I'm just teasing. You want a ride down the street?" I asked.

"Naw, I'm about to smoke; I know you don't," he said, looking all charming.

"You don't know what I do," I said snidely. "But go 'head, I don't need that smell in my mom's car."

"I'll call you when I get back home, a'ight?" he said as he began walking toward the barbershop.

"A'ight," I said after he stopped me and planted a nice long one on my lips. I almost crashed into the car parked next to our driveway before peeling out.

I thought I had an orgasm. That kiss was so good.

I just made it to my appointment, messing around with Love. Stacey eyed me as I jumped in the chair 'cause she didn't play about her time or money.

"I almost took Cindi if you was two more minutes late. You know I don't play about," Stacey began.

I cut her off. "My time or my money," I whined, mimicking her.

She slapped me on the head and began to part my hair to start my relaxer.

I asked Cindi to run next door to the mini-mart for me while Stacey worked this perm in.

"So, are you really cutting all this hair off?" she asked me for the hundredth time.

"Yes, I already told you, it will grow back. I need a change," I said, trying not to sound as irritated as I felt.

I said nothing as I let her wash out the relaxer and condition my hair.

"You know we can do a wig or something?" she pressed the issue further, not wanting to cut the hair she had kept long and healthy since I was a little girl.

"Are you done?" I asked.

She looked at me as she was about to check me, and before she could get the words out, I cut a big section of my hair. She had no choice but to do what I requested. I felt Stacey's eyes again; I knew she wanted to punch the shit out of me, but she just fussed and finished cutting it into the style I requested. That bob was the talk of the school after prom. Stacey got so much business from that hairstyle; she should have given me a cut after all the fuss.

Cindi came back with my Coke and Snyder Bar-B-Q chips. I crushed them as I sat under that dryer for what seemed like a damn eternity, but it was worth it. This bob was so silky and long and cut to perfection. When Stacey was done, I pulled out my Polaroid to capture the moment (I don't know what I did with that pic).

I paid Stacey and headed to Joy's spot to get my nails and toes done. My girl Joy had her own shop not too far from the salon, so I called her to let her know I was on my way. I walked out of the salon. The sun was shining bright. It would be a good day.

I arrived at Venetian on Highland Ave. Joy did her thang on my nails and toes, per usual. She gave me the acrylic tips with her own bomb ass artwork-purple swirl, pink, silver mix... she did her thang! And she matched my toes to the T! I was a very satisfied customer.

We spent the whole time gossiping and talking about her regulars we didn't like. Joy was older than me, but I loved the wisdom and advice she gave without me asking most times. My sis for life.

The heat from the sun lit me up as I exited the salon; I remembered to bring an umbrella, so my hair didn't sweat out. I realized I had enough time for a nap before Khi came to beat this face.

My excitement got the best of me; as well as not wanting to ruin my hair, I could not fall asleep. I flicked through the channels as I lay atop the purple comforter on my daybed.

The Color Purple was just starting to play on BET, and I turned that shit off.

"They will not have me crying in my feelings today."

I turned the cartoons on and watched some Flintstones… I used to love this cartoon when I was younger. Mr. Slate was always on Fred and Barnie's asses; I would've quit if I were them. You ain't talking to me crazy like that all the time.

Just like that, it was 4:30, and I was fast asleep; I didn't even know I had dozed off. I jumped up and ran to the mirror to ensure my hair was still on point. It was, but I still picked up the phone to call Stacey to see if she could touch me up real quick. I heard my mother's voice as I placed the receiver to my ear.

"Martin, please don't bring that woman to my house. This day is for your daughter, and while I bite my tongue any other time, I don't want her over at my house." I overheard my mom say to my father.

"Dina, why do you always have to do this? April is a part of my life now, and I'm not gonna keep making her feel like an outsider because you can't get over the past. I'm sorry things ended the way they did, and it's not April's fault. It's mine. You want to blame someone, blame me, okay? But stop. Today will be the last time I leave her. I'm just preparing you for future interactions. She will be there," he said.

"Kiss my ass, Martin," she said as she slammed the phone.

I made my call to Stacey, and she was able to come through before I left out. I ran downstairs to check on my mom. Since my father left, she just hadn't been able to process the new relationship he had… it'd been years. I vowed not to be her; bitter.

Khi and Stacey arrived simultaneously and put those skills to work. I showered first; I wasn't going to no prom musty, and plus, I didn't know what might happen after prom. I was prepped and ready to go in just enough time to jump in my dress and get a couple of pics before Love arrived. I told Daddy not to embarrass me, which that man had a way of scaring every male I met off.

"You're my baby girl, and I need these knuckle-headed niggas to know that if they hurt you, it will be a problem," Daddy assured me of his why.

I knew not to argue because Daddy meant what he said, and he meant to protect me from any and everyone. I loved him for that.

The doorbell rang as my mom and Stacey helped me put my dress on and fastened the zipper on the back. I began to sweat because that meant Love would be downstairs with my father until I was ready. Mom could see the worry on my face as the doorbell rang for the third time.

"Let me go answer the door." She winked as she descended the stairs.

I heard her greet Love and welcome him in. Then I heard my dad.

"So, what's your name, son?" he asked as he went into grilling Love.

"My name is DeVaughn Lovely, sir."

I heard Love answer him in the politest way I'd ever heard him speak.

"Where you from?" my dad continued.

"I'm originally from Chicago but moved to Pittsburgh when I was 5," he responded.

As Daddy finished his "ask 50 questions," he told him the dos and don'ts with me, and Love responded with a reassuring "Yes, sir."

As I descended the stairs, all eyes were on me. Love's mouth was slightly ajar as he stared intently at my dress. However, Daddy ruined the moment.

"Boy, if you don't pick your damn lip up off this floor!" he scolded Love.

We all laughed as Mommy came to Love's defense. "Martin, if you don't leave this boy alone. Our baby looks beautiful, don't ruin this for her. I mean it!" She continued, "DeVaughn,

I'm sorry if Mr. Bentley is stressing you out, baby. I want you both to have a good time tonight. Just no prom babies."

We looked confused, and then I looked at her like, "Mom!"

"Ain't not one baby being made tonight, oh my gosh!" I exclaimed.

Love opened the door for us to go outside and take pics because the sun was still shining. Once Mom and Daddy finished taking pics, Love drove us to the lineup, where I met his parents and took more pics. I hadn't talked to Camille all day. As soon as we spotted one another, we left our dates running and hugged one another. We doted on how fine the other looked; our parents took pics of us.

Love and Lamar found us, and we took couples pics and a group pic. We grabbed our dates as they announced all prom attendees to the front of the school to be announced.

Camille and Lamar were among the first 20 couples to be announced; I cheered my ass off when they called their names, as well as a couple of other people I knew. Then it was Love and me; I mean, the excitement I felt as we stepped onto the platform and walked out. The smile I gave him as he spun me around so that everyone could see my dress; an A-Line electric purple thing with a plunging neckline and the back out; Love with his black suit with an Electric Purple vest and shoes to match. We looked bomb as hell, I must say. I saw our parents looking so proud.

The rest of the prom was a bit of a blur. I could say for certain that Camille, Lamar, Love and I had a ball. The DJ had us moving *all night*, playing Chubb Rock, MJB, Heavy D, Aliyah, Brandy, Prince, Biggie, and SWV. Lamar and Love left Camille and me on the dance floor after we danced to "Forever My Lady" by Jodeci. If we love nothing else, we love to dance. I remember Javon and Nique (her real name was Ronnique) winning prom king and queen. The last songs of the night were Poison by BBD. As the lights came up, the DJ played "Sound Boy Killing 'Em," and Love and Lamar had to pull us off the dance floor; *the* best night ever! No, Love ain't get nowhere near the cookies. He got to work for these (wink).

After graduation, I attended college at Morgan State University in Baltimore, Maryland and Camille at Howard University in Washington, D.C. I didn't get to see Love until I was home on breaks, and sometimes not even then 'cause our lives took two different paths. Let's just say his university was called Hard Knocks, and the streets were his professors. It would be years until we would see one another again.

I missed Camille. She was a gem to my life (besides therapy), sort of like a rainbow to my cloud. We were inseparable from middle to high school. She was the brown sugar beauty that all the guys liked. Her mane was natural, and she was the only female I knew who not only rocked it low but dyed it any color and looked *haute*! That was my sis!

I guess people are in your life for a reason, a season, or a lifetime; she and I lasted many seasons. Camille came into my life in the winter months of my life, which lasted until we graduated. I am forever grateful for her. Not that we never spoke again, but our lives went in different directions once we graduated from high school.

Camille knew all my secrets—things I couldn't tell everyone. I never felt protection from the adults in my life. It had always been my peers, Jason and Camille, who I told everything, really. She even knew that I was being molested by my older cousin, Jay. My mother knew, too, but she never protected me; she was the reason I never told my father.

They were the people I felt safe with, although Camille had more information than Jason. As I said, he was hella crazy, and he would have killed Jay for touching me. I remember this boy in middle school touching my butt, and I hit him. He wanted some girls to fight me after Jason finished dusting his ass in front of the entire grade; he and those girls never touched me.

Camille knew my need to be seen and being flirtatious was all because of what I'd been through. She didn't down me or see me as a ho, like my mom or most of the females at school did. Who knew to escape the pain from one thing will bring pain from another direction? I dressed nicely, kept myself up and just loved myself even more that I guess I came off as conceited to the females at school. They had no idea I did it not to sink into the depression that they were now causing.

I fought hard not to succumb to the mental drain and not to cut myself like I did due to the abuse.

Camille moved to California after graduating from Howard. She does marketing for a prestigious music label and she's doing well for herself. We connect via phone and social media, and we take yearly girls' trips. When we meet up, sometimes it is like we never skipped a beat.

I had been sensing something had changed. I just couldn't put my finger on it.

Camille Carter

"Hard times will always reveal true friends."
— Anonymous

Since seventh grade, I've held it down for Nikki, being her shoulder to cry on when her cousin assaulted her. When her parents would fight, I would sneak her into my room until morning. However, as we grew, secretly, I started to hate that bitch. I didn't know when it started, but I just began to see her as a conceited, self-centered, lack of self-awareness and accountability ass bitch who looked out for no one but herself—or only for others *if* it benefitted her in some way. Yeah, we remain friends and get together, and I know I am not being true to myself or this friendship. Something has to be done, but first.

How did we get here? I know I am her children's godparent, but during my time apart from her and developing other friendships, I realized I was more of a friend to her than she was to me, which is my own fault. In therapy, I've learned that I have a hard time with conflict and saying "no." It makes me angry that there were times she set up double dates for *us*, but she was the one who wanted the date. I was the tag along because she didn't want to go alone. Don't get me wrong, as a friend, you should look out for your friends, but Nikki dropped the ball on me a couple of times to the point I have the opinion I have of her now.

When we were in college, I was dating no good motherfucking Raymond (he was the finest Kappa on campus, and he knew it (red flag #1)). I found out on my own after six months of dating him that he had a habit of "making" his women do what he wanted by physical force.

One night at a Kappa party, he told me he'd meet me at the party, which was at his frat house, because he had to work. When he walked into the party, he saw me dancing with one of his frat brothers, Robert, and turned into a green-eyed bandit. He snatched me by my arm so quickly that my head jolted from the force. His line brother tried to calm him down and tell him it was just a dance, but he either dismissed what he said or didn't hear him.

All I knew was when he pushed me into a room in the frat house, he wailed at me. He slapped me in the face and then punched me in the stomach repeatedly until I fell to the floor sobbing. I begged him to stop, but he ignored my pleas and told me how much of a whore I was and how I disrespected him as he continued to punch me all over my body. The body parts you couldn't see received the most damage, especially my heart and spirit. When he felt I had been punished enough, he left the room to go back to the party like nothing had ever happened.

I lay there nearly lifeless as Nikki, who happened to be visiting me for the weekend, and Robert looked for me after he returned to the party. Nikki asked him where I was, and he pointed down the hall. They must've checked every room until they found me.

Nikki rushed to me like, "Sis, are you okay?!"

The groans I released as she and Robert tried to help me up let her know I was in bad shape.

Here was where I took offense with her; she said, "Girl, you better than me. I would have whooped his ass if it was me." Then she proceeded to encourage me not to file charges because it wouldn't do me any good. It would be my word against his.

I resented her for that dumb-ass advice. No, I never discussed it, but it did make me think twice about the person I called "sis" and "friend."

The straw that broke the camel's back was when I had just been diagnosed with Stage 1 breast cancer in 2001. I had recently moved to California after graduating. When I left the doctor's office, I was in disbelief.

"How could this be happening to me?" I asked God.

I think I went through all the stages of grief in those 5 minutes I sat in my car. I had to get myself together to go to the grocery store and pick up something for dinner. I no longer had the desire to cook, but I needed to distract myself from this news. After I purchased my things for what I felt was my last meal, I sat in the grocery store parking lot contemplating suicide.

I know you're thinking, "Sis, it's not the end of the world. It's stage 1," so all hope is not lost. After what I had been through with my depression diagnosis after my experience with Raymond, which I've not spoken about freely, this news was the tip of the iceberg for me. With depression, little uncontrollable things could cause me great distress and instant reactions and not a response.

So, I decided to call Nikki and cry my eyes out to her. Instead, I was met with an annoyed response, like she couldn't take my crying into the phone. When she answered the phone and heard my voice shake, all she could say was, "Sis, quit crying. It ain't the end of the world. You can cry, or you can fight. Which one will you do?"

My reply was, "I'ma do both." I hung up. She didn't call me back either.

After the incident with Raymond, I felt I knew where I stood with her and moved accordingly. I used her like I felt she was using me. Catching rides home, if my phone ran out of minutes, I'd use hers, borrowing outfits and not returning them, only calling when I needed something; I guess that was the Scorpio in me. I thank God I had changed since then and reconciled with my sis, but for a long time, I hated that bitch.

In 2019, she came out to Los Angeles to visit, as she always did. We were catching up and reminiscing about the good ol' days. She mentioned that she had seen Raymond, and he walked right past her like he never knew her.

With a raised eyebrow, I asked, "Why would he do that?"

Nikki told me that night after he pulverized me, she vowed to avenge my honor. Basically, she got some D.C. dudes to whoop his ass real good before she returned to Morgan. She told him if he *ever* touched a woman the way he did her sis, she'd have him killed. He graduated and was never heard from again.

When she shared this with me, I realized that love protects, and you may not even be aware of it until years later. I had to come clean to her and let her know how I felt until I heard this.

I also confessed to her things I did while in college. Nikki cried as she asked me to forgive her. She explained that she couldn't deal with my diagnosis at that time, being that she had just lost her nana to the disease; she never grieved that loss. My revelation just uncovered that pain.

"I know that's not an excuse for not being there for you, but that is the only way I could handle your news at that time. Please forgive me, sis."

She and I are in a much better place now because of it. As it is said, "The truth makes you free."

Nikki said she wished she had known how I felt sooner because she sensed there was something was amidst with us, but she couldn't put her finger on it. She apologized for being a bitch and thinking of herself; she was in her work of self-discovery and realized she used taking from others the way she did as a coping mechanism for her own trauma and pain, which she had been addressing.

She told me, "Sis, me, you, we. We are a work in progress. We'll get through this *together*."

I'm so glad she is so positive and sees things from a "things will get better" perspective. I have always admired her for that. Though she has gone through what she's gone through, her spirit to persevere has never died. That's my sis forever.

Love is patient and kind; it is not jealous
or conceited or proud;
Love is not ill-mannered
or selfish or irritable;
Love does not keep a record of wrongs;
Love is not happy with evil but is happy
with the truth. Love never gives up; and
its faith, hope, and patience never fail.
Love is ETERNAL.

I Corinthians 13:4–8a (GNT)

The Get Down

"One day the right kind of love will find you, and it will be at the right time. It will be when you need it most."

– R.M. Drake

They say that the right kind of love will find you at the right time when you need it most. I'm not so sure of that because I found love, and so much was going on in my life, but I knew it was love. It felt right at the wrong time, but right, nonetheless.

Work was busy. So many callers with emotions that I just couldn't deal with on this particular day. I had already come to work with an attitude because Essex, my on-and off-again live-in boyfriend and children's father and I had gotten into another argument, which ended with him gaslighting me about confronting him cheating, yet again. I didn't know why I kept putting myself through that; I knew the relationship was toxic, but I was so stuck on the familiar that I couldn't find the courage to leave then.

5:00 pm came, and I speed walked down Forbes, through the bustle of the downtown streets, to get home to a glass of wine. As I approached my bus stop, I recognized a familiar face. It was DeVaughn Lovely! I hadn't seen him in years. Something about him still made me weak.

Was Love supposed to be this damn gorgeous (can you call a man that?)? Forget what Love did… damn, Love was still *fawineee!*

Until that sunny summer day, I had kindly declined Love's pursuit. I think Thotisha took over that day cause I was like, "Bump it, you only live once." Yeah, I know, I know. I should be killing my flesh, but she won that day. Whatever I didn't allow to happen as Seniors or those free summers, weeell (shoulder shrug), I let the chips fall where they may this day. I could say I didn't know what made me entertain his advances this day, but I did, and I didn't regret any of the events that transpired.

Love was sexy, charming and gave the appearance of a hard-working man these days, and I fell for him all over again. As I approached the bus stop to go home, our eyes met as if some cosmic alignment had occurred for us to see one another. They say the eyes are the window to the soul. Those eyes had lust written all over them, as did mine, but that was not the point. How did I know his eyes were full of lust? I'd been on this earth too long *not* to know. You know the way you look at a brother who walks into a room looking like he has the confidence of your favorite celebrity; it's that look.

Love's five-foot-eleven dark chocolate frame was posted up, licking his lips as I walked up to the bus stop, and our eyes met. The way he called my name (as he always did every time he saw me), with that sultry tone that said, "I want you", made me weak, but I could never show him that. When he called me, you would've thought I had some exotic name, but anything out of his mouth seduced me. His swag was a trait that made the butterflies in my stomach flutter. I knew this feeling all too well, and what should have been a red flag, I entertained.

As we took our seats on the bus ride home, he sat in front of me and smiled; he gave off the confidence of a man who knew he could bag a woman. It was not cocky or awkward; it was confident and sexy as fuck.

It had been a while since we'd seen one another long enough to catch up, so here we were, seated for twenty minutes, catching up. What I thought was catching up was him telling me things he had never had the opportunity to share with me on all the summer breaks from college—he really wanted me to be his. He started telling me how I broke his heart, and I asked him how.

He said, "You went and got married on me."

I didn't bother to tell him I had been divorced and was just in a long-term relationship. My first marriage lasted two minutes. I'm embellishing, but we were young and thought we were in love. You learn early that love doesn't pay bills or cover up abuse.

He went on to say how he always loved me. I, with my smart mouth, corrected him and told him it was lust. My words had no effect on his ego. He knew exactly what he meant to say, and it drew me in more. Now I was thinking to myself, this was the type of man I liked, paid me no attention when I said something smart 'cause shit like this would occur daily with me. However, I didn't want to jump to a conclusion that might not even occur, so I chilled and listened and entertained our flirtatious convo like we always had.

Every time I saw Love over the years, he gave me that look. You know the look that you give something that you can't wait to have, like an over-anticipated gift. That lustful eye you give that one thing you know you either can't or shouldn't have, but you just want to know what it feels like, tastes like, smells like.

That thing you desire sits, and it appears saying, "I'm all yours when you're ready."

Yeah, that was the vibe I was getting, but again, I had to keep my composure. I didn't want to appear like my thoughts, Thotisha… she a freak. Thotisha needed to let him believe she wasn't as interested as she was. I couldn't believe I, one, let him get away and, two, ain't give him none in high school. Still, I wouldn't allow that shit to happen again… I *promise* you that.

So, we are on the bus, and I tell him he never told me he wanted to pursue a relationship with me. He refreshed my memory by telling me he wanted to be with me a couple of years back. I was amazed because the men I'd entertained couldn't remember shit. I do remember him saying that; I paid him no mind, like all the other times, because one, I was in a relationship, two, he grew to be a man they said was "for the streets" (from what the streets were saying) and three, I certainly believed he didn't want anything serious from this situationship. Although it seemed that ship might have sailed, I was willing to steer the sail back in his direction.

When a man could tell you what he told you, and you both could remember how that conversation went, man, that was sexy. I had some real lying ass niggas in my life. What he recalled made me believe that he really was still interested. The consistency in his statements toward me and about me sealed the deal. Being in the relationships I'd been in; you look for holes in niggas' stories. He appeared trustworthy from my *ID*, *Fatal Attraction*, and *First 48* watching self.

Go ahead and laugh, but niggas be out here not remembering what they did 24 hours ago (let them tell it). You know, a man who will say one thing and do another? They will lie, get caught in a lie and still want you to believe they are honest and faithful, not Love. To have someone like Love tell you what they told you six years ago can make your inner parts quite excited. At this point, Thotisha was roaring to come out.

At the moment, I fell for him, hook, line and sinker, and I wasn't turning back, more so now than I did in high school. I was in a transition, feeling depressed, oppressed, and just wanting to be free of what I had been experiencing. Seeing how those who wanted to keep me in their "Nikki stay good box" had done some messed up things that involved my feelings and trust, I was looking for Love to be more of an escape from all of that than just a good time. No, Love was my rebellion against all I had experienced. I figured, "They all did what they wanted to do, and so will I," so I did, with Love.

We exchanged numbers, and I hit him up as I arrived home. I called, and he answered, and we talked about how this arrangement would work out. He asked if he should call or wait for my call. I told him maybe I'd just call him. We decided on our first meet-up that same week. Call me whatever you want, but don't call me late for dinner because I had already decided that when we met, he was getting the cookie, no if, ands or buts about it.

Later that week, I was out walking and hit him up and asked if he wanted to meet at a local park. He suggested I come to his spot. I agreed and plugged his address into the GPS. No lie, I was trying to talk myself out of it by praying. I did talk to God and asked him to mess up my plans because I was going to meet this man, and I was going to give him the cookie. Now usually, God listened when I spoke prayers like this and made something occur so that it foiled my plans to let me know I shouldn't be doing no fucked up shit like this.

Guess where my ass ended up? Yup, right at his front door. The rest was history or the future, however you want to look at it. He welcomed me into his place as if he had been waiting to welcome his woman home from work. I grinned and kissed him passionately as he led me into his spacious abode. I had never seen a guy's home so immaculate with pictures around the walls; he had a hell of a taste for the finer things in life. The pale blue accent wall of his living room had photos of his five children on it ranging from oldest to youngest. The frames were trimmed in silver. He even had pictures of his parents and siblings strategically placed atop his glass-topped coffee and end tables. Not a smudge of dust in sight; I couldn't even say that for myself. I sat down next to him on his mahogany-colored leather couch, and he pulled me in closer to him, saying, "My baby's home now."

I didn't know how to take him. Should I play into it or reject the statement so that no emotional attachments were made from what was about to take place? I rejected it with silence and a smile, or so I thought.

Love said, "God brought us back together," as he poured some libations for us to indulge in.

I couldn't allow myself to agree with his statement because we were both in a relationship. I had been raised to believe God would not bring you someone else's mate nor take you to someone if you had a mate, right? I know it was cliché, but what else was I to believe about what I was experiencing at that moment? Remember, as a good girl, I shouldn't have had myself in this situation, yet there I was. Trying to make sense of this vibe I was feeling, something that felt so good and peaceful couldn't have been wrong, right? Love found me at what I believed was the wrong time, but it felt so damn good.

I had this dream. I rarely remember my dreams, but where I was now was like déjà vu, and it was very eerie to me. The dream I began to remember while hanging out with Love was action-packed. People were shooting at me, and I was trying to get away, so I entered a vehicle with an unknown man, and I lay my head on his chest, as if I belonged there. This person gave me peaceful vibes, freedom from what I was dealing with and a sense of security. We were driven away from the chaos and into a ball of fire. As I sat there with Love, I sensed he was my unknown man, that safe place. He was in my dream... However, he was taken, and so was I... and that was what didn't make sense.

I attempted to push that thought to the back of my mind because I wanted to enjoy my night with Love. Trying to permit myself to be fully present because, in the back of my mind, this shouldn't even be happening, but did I get up and walk out? Hell no! Why? Because being with Love just felt right at the moment and the moments that we shared after that evening. He brought a feeling of peace and calmness I'd not experienced, probably ever, in my life. As I look back on it, maybe he was the oasis to the turmoil I was facing, and, at that moment, I wanted that to last.

We sat on his sofa, had some drinks, talked about our high school days and prom, and let the ID channel watch us.

"I don't remember a lot from the prom after the lineup," I confessed.

"Oh, I remember it all. Bridget and Camille got into it because Bridge wanted to dance with Lamar, and Camille was not having it." He laughed.

"I do not remember that." I felt really small not remembering this detail about Camille, and she never mentioned it.

"Yeah, I know Camille was gonna put hands on her until you stepped in," he reminded me.

Love reminded me of the *Soul Train* line Gina started, and everyone was dancing all night.

"That's probably why I don't remember. I was on the floor all night."

"I had to drag your ass off when it was time to go! You was trying to have your dad hunt me down, weren't you?" he teasingly asked.

Laughing, I said with a tone that let him know that I admired that, "I do remember that he grilled the hell out of you, but you stood your ground."

I sat and listened as he told me about his experiences of being on the streets and doing time in jail for doing dumb shit after graduation. As I listened intently, everything about him seemed so genuine and transparent. I could listen to him all damn day. Nothing was better than listening to someone who had taken life's lemons and made lemonade and lived to tell you about it. Love continued to tell me how he changed his life around, not wanting to go back to jail and beginning to do something with his life by opening his own contracting business.

Most companies don't hire people with records, especially black men. The fact that he created his own when no one wanted to hire him spoke volumes about his drive and motivation to make lemonade; again, I was turned on immensely.

We talked until the liquor was talking for us, then it happened. He kissed me with his full and soft lips. I kissed him back, and our tongues wanted to see who could beat who down the other's throat; I won. I proceeded to disrobe him, and he stopped me, not because he didn't want me, but to take me to his room.

Taking my hand, he said, "Come with me. I have a more comfortable place for you," as he led me to the bedroom. I followed him up the dark staircase, holding his hand tightly. He laughed at the pressure I applied.

"Don't tell me you're afraid of the dark?" he teased.

"I'm in an unfamiliar place, in the dark, my guy, so yes, I'm a little scared," I said.

"I got you," he said with such believable confidence.

I eased up my grip on his hand. He turned on the lamp to give me a better view of his room. I almost believed Love loved more than just me cause this room was amazing. Look like some shit off *MTV Cribs*; the décor was beautiful! I didn't even bother to ask if his woman did this 'cause sis was not on my list of people to thank right now.

After Love grabbed my waist and pulled me toward him, the shit got real, really quickly. Gently and seductively, he began to kiss my lips, then my neck, as he was steadily raising my shirt until he stepped back to help me out of it. While he was at it, I popped the bra 'cause I was ready as a motherfucker.

He excused himself as he entered the attached bathroom to prepare himself for what was about to go down. As he was in the bathroom, I stepped out of my distressed jeans and purple laced panties, holding nothing back for when he exited the bathroom. He opened the door and saw me butt-ass naked on his bed. He took a minute to admire what he saw before he walked over to put in work.

As he walked towards me, he said, "Alexa, play 'When We' by Tank."

I chimed in and said, "Alexa, play 'All I' by Jill Scott," and the first of many love sessions were started.

Sparing you the details, but the tongue was fire. The passion was there, but I didn't know. Something was missing. I didn't complain or say anything negative; I just let him hold me like that shit was amazing. I waited 20 fucking years for this bullshit! The kisses and passion are what kept me coming back because, for me, it just had to get better. We talked some before I left, and I never mentioned the lack of performance. I decided to enjoy the time we spent. I took a shower and dressed; he helped me with my bra. I knew this was a regular thing for him cause this man fastened my shit quicker than I could. I let it slide 'cause I knew what we were and what we were not going to be at this point.

Over the next couple of months, Love and I texted in between our random encounters. Still, the performance improved tremendously. That last time was the last time; I told myself I would end what we had going on. It wasn't going anywhere, and I started to catch feelings for something that was just a fuck.

I ended it after our last hotel rendezvous. I think his lady knew something was up. She would stay home more, so we just changed our meet-up spot. I must say, that was the most amazing sex I'd had! It improved greatly! The chair, shower, whew… I did things with Love I had not done with Essex, ever. He brought the sexy feminine energy that was bottled up inside of me out.

As amazing as it was, I knew I had to end it. I had some business ventures Essex and I were getting into, and I wanted to keep my head clear moving forward, but it was too late. I found out I was pregnant three months after cutting things off with Love; so much for cutting things off.

As a courtesy, I tried calling him to inform him of my pregnancy, but he changed his number and deleted his social media accounts. I was furious that he would take my ending things so personally, that he would really not fuck with me for real; what an asshole! I didn't want to reach out to his family or mutual friends because no one knew we were involved, so I kept a low profile.

I guess it was this baby and me. I had to tell Essex, and he was pissed but willing to stay. I ended things with him as well. Our relationship had run its course, and the pregnancy had proven that. He and I both knew things were not working out. There were more bad days than good days, and I did not want one more pregnancy being stressed out over a nigga that really wasn't for me.

Essex was and still is a forgiving dude, but I realized he was not "my person." He was a support during my pregnancy. I appreciated him for that.

Love

"She is the kind of fire that needs a warning label: Dangerous for the heart and highly addictive."
— Albert Alexander Bukoski

Nicole Bentley, a.k.a. Nikki, a.k.a Ms. Fine as Hell. Damn, hadn't seen her since last year or the year before that.

I was taking my mom shopping at Adage, one of the local grocery stores. She looked fine as always, with her braids swinging and landing right above her booty; boy, did she have one! She had on a blue jogging suit with some matching blue shoes. I remember her being like that in school, always matching. As I daydreamed about being with her, I thought, "What're my chances of running into her fine ass of all days like today?" Maybe today was the day I'd really shoot my shot.

I'd liked this woman since high school, but for various reasons, we just didn't date. If I could be deep, I didn't believe she would want to be with a guy like me.

See, we were drastically different in how we were raised. She seemed more loved at home and didn't engage in what the females around me did; you know, "that ho shit," letting every ninja in the neighborhood run up in them. She was that nu-nu type, suburban with a little bit of hood, with enough personality to try and test where she was on the ho spectrum. Yeah, men have a ho spectrum; we gauge what girl will give it up on the spot and which will make you wait for it. Nikki was the one to tease you and make you wait.

I remember she and her homegirls were walking down the street on my end of the block, and they stopped to talk to the fellas and me. Her girl was dating my homeboy at the time. I stepped to her in my regular flirty way, and she didn't reject me as I thought she would. I stole a kiss and tried to touch her booty, but she smacked my arm away. Then proceeded to glide her hand against my jawn as her crew moved past us; she turned back and winked at me mischievously. I knew that one day, I'd see where the next kiss and rub would go. She was the good girl type, but we all know what good girls could do when given the right charm and environment. I wanted to know first-hand what she was capable of. I was a patient man.

"I'll have my day," I'd always told myself and didn't know that day, when we happened to run into one another, was my day—my time had come.

We were products of our environment, whether we admitted it or not. How we reacted, spoke, ate, thought, and even the emotion we showed were from our environment. Our environment might have shown us the negative or the positive, but it gave us what it thought was right in navigating through life. When someone came along and interrupted our standard, you never forgot. I remember Nikki from that day and made sure with minimum effort that she was a part of my life in some form or fashion during high school. However, my environment took me in another direction.

I grew up around drug dealing, drug using, gangs, fast girls, church, and a lot of shit that shaped who I was and the choices I made to bring me to where I was now. I'd kept my ear to the streets about Nikki and knew she graduated college and had a couple of kids. I still thought about her and what could have been. She was one of the sweetest and kindest women I'd met.

The relationships I'd had since high school were toxic and unproductive. The only thing good that came from them was my children. Thankfully, I didn't create a lot of little humans to provide for, and I had a good relationship with them; their mothers, now, that was a different story for some of them. I got one that made me wish I would have dead some shit that should have never lived, like the toxic relationship I had with Melissa. Being reconnected to Nikki, that deferred dream might be about to come to pass.

I had some business to handle in the city and didn't want to pay that high ass parking fee, so I took the bus. As I was sitting at the bus stop to go back home, I looked around, and who did I see? Nikki was coming my way.

Her eyes met mine, and she gave me a flirtatious sultry contact that gave me the mental fist bump to go head and holla at her. I remained calm as she came over to me and gave me a hug. It wasn't that raggedy church hug females be giving out when they didn't like you. You know, the one when they embrace from the side and pat you on the shoulder? That whack shit, but it wouldn't have stopped my mission.

When she wrapped her arms around my waist 'cause she was just a little thing compared to my towering frame, I could smell her perfume. It was so appealing, and I wanted her to stay in my arms for a few more minutes. I complimented her on her perfume and asked what it was.

She said, "Seduction," with a sheepish grin, like she had some capacity to know she would see me and lure me in as she always had. Well, it worked, and that was my cue to put it out there, let her know my interest and see what comes of it.

Now, don't get me wrong, I had confidence as a man. I could pull women, but Nikki was different. She had literally been the one not to take the shit that I talked about back in the day, so I knew if I wanted that chance, I needed to come correct. As we waited for whatever bus she was catching, I let her know that she broke my heart.

She looked at me puzzled and said, "How?" She said, "I never knew that. You never told me."

I had to remind her of the time, a couple of years back, when I expressed to her, while she was on vacation, of wanting to date her. She looked at me and grinned. She updated me that she was still in that relationship.

I simply told her, "I don't give a fuck about that. I'm trying to be with you."

She waved me off like I was playing, but I was serious as hell. I wanted to show her just how serious I was as I pulled her toward me and laid one right on her lips. She was stunned and looked embarrassed, but I didn't give a fuck; I wasn't gonna let her think I was playing like all the other times.

The bus came, and we paid our fare. I took a seat in front of her as we chatted, and I soaked in her beauty. Nikki had an aura about her that made men just want to see what she was about. Now here I was, falling victim to her innocent seduction. She wore the right perfume 'cause, man! Never mind, you feel me.

My emotions went from high to low, but it didn't stop me from giving her my number and getting hers as we took our seats on the not-so-crowded bus. Her current relationship must not be too good if she was throwing me her number, I thought to myself. This just boosted my confidence 'cause, for one, if her man were doing her right, she wouldn't be entertaining me as she was, and, two, she damn sure wouldn't have given me her number or taken mine.

I could say the same for myself. I had been with Melissa for the past five years out of convenience and obligation. She was a jump-off I ended up getting pregnant. I was not a man to disregard my responsibilities, so I stayed and made the best of it. Our son, Dior, was the best thing that had come from this relationship (or lack of it). Melissa had two other children, and as the relationship progressed, she showed a lack of maturity and respect for the other fathers and me; that rubbed me the wrong way. Melissa was what one would call a "bitter bitch." I didn't use that word for females, but she was. She was as hoodrat as they came, and I fell for the okie doke. Naw, I wouldn't lay the blame solely on her. She had a fat ass, and it didn't take me long to get the panties. In my immature era, this was what I did, hit it and quit it, but a few times, those hits resulted in a child, and she was one.

Soon after she had Dior, she would start tripping about me coming home late and saying I wasn't there for our son. She compared me to the rest of her "raggedy ass baby daddies"(her words, not mine). I was sitting here taking care of her and my child, and I know for a damn fact a couple of her children's fathers were taking care of their children. Yet all she saw was what we weren't doing for her, not our children. I soon learned she was selfish and self-centered, and that didn't sit well with me.

While I didn't have my father in my life all the time, he was present and taught me what a man should be for his children, and my mother never talked badly about him or any of my other siblings' fathers. After five years of dealing with that and her not changing, I had to let this relationship go, even if she got petty and wouldn't let me see my son.

I finally asked her to move out a month ago; because she was so petty, the day I ran into Nikki was the day I came from Family Court for child support and custody. Melissa was madder than a motherfucker when the judge set the support amount based on what I was already doing and gave me joint custody. 'Cause one thing this woman would *never* say was I was a deadbeat. So, seeing Nikki was a prize to my day. Yeah, Melissa would probably be back over at some point but for right now, I would enjoy Nikki's fine ass and see where this might go.

Nikki gave me enough about her relationship to know the door to her heart was open for visitors; I vowed to be its first guest. Honestly, if I could rethink my intentions, I must say that Nikki was more than I wanted to deal with. Maybe it was my own insecurities about not taking the same opportunities we were both given, but I knew she was a catch. I just wasn't ready for what she had to bring to the table. She was an author, public speaker, mentor, and active in her community, church and other organizations; I was not. She made me want to be, to be with her, though, and perhaps that was what scared me… Success.

We talked that same week and planned to meet up. Melissa and I were no longer living together, and so I decided to invite Nikki out. If things went as I imagined, we'd end the night at my place. Don't be mad, 'cause if you saw Nikki, you'd know why my mind went there first. I waited years to hit it.

She reached out to me one day and wanted to meet up. I invited her over, and I just had a feeling that things would go down. Let's just say she was all that I had imagined.

I didn't expect that I would be hitting the drawls so early, but hell, that was what I had been waiting for and apparently, so was she. We caught up on life while she had a couple of drinks and watched tv until it watched us. I have to say, it caught me off guard cause Nikki wasn't the hos I had been talking about. She was the wifey type, with "tendencies" that make you want to wife her. I needed to know where this would go outside of the bedroom.

Our first outing was to a local bar, really low-key.

She teased as she entered the place. "Is this where you take all ya sneaky links?" she asked as she caressed my leg and sat beside me.

"Naw, I could've taken you somewhere else, but I thought this would be good for you since you're the one in the relationship."

"Oh, okay, thanks for thinking about me and my situation," she said.

"What you drinkin'?"

She asked the bartender for a shot of Patron as I admired her beauty in the dimly lit setting.

"Long day for you, babe?" I asked.

"Yeah, something like that, plus they don't have my Strawberry Hennessy, so I settle for this," she said as the bartender handed her the drink, and I paid.

"What are you drinking?" she asked.

"Rum and Coke. About the only thing I do drink. Why do you want one?" I asked.

"Sure," she replied.

"Can I get two rum and Cokes?" I asked the bartender as I felt Nikki out, seeing where life had taken her. From what I could see, it hadn't treated her badly at all.

After a couple of drinks and her talking with some other patrons, we left. She was tipsy and feeling all over me, and I wasn't going to take advantage of her, but I wanted to see where this night would lead. I asked her if she was okay to drive, and she said yes. I told her to follow me, and we'd go to my house. It wasn't that far away. She did well when she followed me and parked behind me in my driveway. She appeared more intoxicated than she drove cause she staggered a bit, meeting me at the steps.

Now she was in my house, in my room, in my bed, and I didn't want to mess this up. I inhaled her scent as she lay next to me. As I held her in my arms, I didn't want this moment to end, but our situations made that decision for us. Damn, why'd it have to be like this? Right person, wrong time. I couldn't even touch her the way I wanted to because I wanted our first time to be where both of us knew exactly what was happening. I didn't want no female saying that I "Bill Cosbyed" or "R. Kellyed" her. Nope, I was not and would never be that guy.

I let her sleep in as I made her breakfast in bed. I never did no shit like this for a woman, and don't y'all go telling nobody about this either. I must say, it felt like this was supposed to happen, she was supposed to be here, and I was just supposed to make love to her differently. Women crave intimacy and not just a fuck; give her that, and the lovemaking will be more than you expected, trust me.

Nikki woke up in a fog and still a bit hung over. She rushed out of bed.

I let her know, "The bathroom is straight ahead," as she dashed to release everything from the night before.

I went and knocked on the door to make sure she was okay after five minutes. She said she was, and I let her know I made breakfast for her to put something on her stomach. Then she repeated her convo with the toilet. I thought, "She did say she was a lightweight." I started laughing cause she was gone after three drinks.

"What's so funny?" she asked while lifting her face from the commode for a minute.

"You and ya lightweight ass; you wasn't lying," I laughed.

"I told you. But I was trying to be grown, and this is what happens when you try to be grown." She turned on the faucet to wash her hands.

I knocked on the bathroom door, even though it was slightly ajar, to hand her a wash rag and towel. She washed her face and stepped out of the bathroom, trying to be as cool about her hangover as possible. That just made me laugh harder. I didn't think she liked that, but the shit was funny.

"Here, eat up with ya drunk ass," I laughingly said as I handed her a plate with eggs, grits, bacon and toast.

"I didn't know you could cook," she stated as she nibbled on the food.

"My moms taught me and my brothers a 'lil something. You would know if you checked in with a brother when you was home from school, you'd know this," I said and winked at her.

"You were out there in them streets. I needed to be focused. That's why I didn't come around," she explained.

"I can respect that. Wasn't nothing out there for you anyway," I say protectively.

"Wasn't nothing out there for you either," she replied.

I didn't know if she was thinking what I was thinking because all I thought was she was damn right. Nothing was out there for me because what was for me was working on her goals while I was dreaming about mine during that time.

Love Wins

"…She's moving differently,
and the price is going up.
She isn't afraid to leave anyone behind.
She's authentic and courageous.
She's the type of woman most pray for
but get intimidated by because she knows
exactly what she wants…"

— Author Unknown

Sometimes You Want What You Want

Sometimes you want more than another person is able, willing, or ready to give to you. It's up to you to realize that and hang in there or move on.

Knowing nothing would come of it, he sure gave the talk that he was all in, always had been. I fell for it, hook, line, and sinker… my fucking feelings, wanting someone to show the kind of care and concern I craved, but knowing in my gut this nigga was lying like a mug. Those beautiful lies I tried hard to dismiss, but part of me craved the affirmations and subtle little things he said to get me aroused and secretly bought into. I hoped I didn't show him that. I tried to curb everything he said with, "You ain't got to say all that," but he insisted on feeding me the beautiful petals of deception I willingly ate. He thought I needed to hear that to get what we both wanted, so unnecessary.

Why do men do that? All you have is "You're so beautiful", "I always thought…", "If you were my woman," when all you really want is… the panties; I mean, what's inside. You have nothing else to say once you get what you want, so why not be honest and forget the pleasantries? Still, I digress.

Silently, I prayed that he would desire me more than just the bedtime romance he was giving. I thought he had grown so used to banging random women, and they allowed it. Why should he settle for commitment when he didn't have to? I was among the casualties.

As I scrolled social media, I was drawn to a video of a relationship coach, Raymond Gaskins, discussing how a woman would know when a man was into her. I thought about Love and his inability to at least "hit me up" like he said he would since our last night together, but he didn't. Then, I knew for sure what this was all about. I knew before, but I low-key deceived myself into thinking that our conversations about "always" liking me, being young and dumb (which we all were), and if I had married him first, he would have given me five babies: one every year. Listen, I tell y'all no lie. It was sexy because I didn't sense he was lying. However, I did tell him, "Those lies are beautiful."

The way Love spoke made me believe he had matured and wanted to have a relationship. He called himself Hubby #2. Ray Gaskins' video pretty much took a needle to my balloon of hope when he said, "A man will seek you out when he wants you. He will make sacrifices to be with you." It'd been three weeks since I saw or spoke to Love. I wasn't calling or texting him either because I didn't want him to think I was Jonesing for him. I believed that he was not that into me. Couldn't a woman have a happy ending to her fantasy?

So, while my heart waited for Love to show interest, here came Carlos. This nigga called out of nowhere, wanting to make plans like I was his woman. What I wanted to say was, "Sir, you got me fucked up. I'm not at all into you." Plus, his ass got 10 damn kids; I was not interested in giving him eleven.

I tried to play nice because society taught women not to bruise men's egos, but this nigga was about to get it. I liked what I liked (I had a type). Don't get me wrong, Carlos was a good guy, but he was allegedly engaged. What he failed to realize was that I was a whole taken woman when it came to him.

The only thing he spoke about was how beautiful I was and how he liked how I dressed. Oh, and how he wanted to eat my ass and kiss both my lips. Now he had assisted me with jitney rides and things like that, but the vibe I got from him was suspect. When I felt that way, I was good, and he was friend-zoned in my head. His flirtatious texts were left on read.

Carlos reminded me of the guy (Michael) in *Waiting to Exhale* who was all over Lela Rochon's character, Robin, and couldn't last when it came to the bedroom. Then, all of a sudden, he tried to play her because she was no longer interested. In contrast, I could care less if he played me. Still, just the way Michael was all over her was how I felt about this dude, and I didn't like that. Carlos was too fucking clingy without ever getting the cookie. That was a turn-off for me.

Unbeknownst to me, Carlos and Love knew each other from the job site. They would talk until they discovered they were talking about the same woman—me. I didn't know how I became the topic of discussion. Love later told me that Carlos was showing him a pic of me (stolen from social media) talking about the woman he'd have. Love said he laughed and showed him a selfie he had of us. Now both these fools wanted to see who I'd pick over the other. That choice wouldn't be hard.

After months of not communicating, Carlos texted me out of the blue one day, a general "Hello, how ya been?"

I knew once I saw it, I should have left his ass on read because no sooner than I did respond, he said, "We should link up soon."

It'd been stated to him many a time that I was in a relationship, but it never stopped him from wanting to make plans with me. Carlos had even offered to cook for me, just walk and take a trip to Chicago, but I always let him down nicely as not to hurt his feelings.

No sooner did Carlos text me, here came Love with his "Good morning, babe, how's your day going?"

I affectionately replied, "Morning, Love, it's great. How's yours?" I knew I was a damn hypocrite, but there was something about Love that made me respond differently and without shame.

Even my current guy, Essex, didn't make me feel secure like Love did. Was that sad? Essex and I had many breakups, and he never came with the affection and attention Love had. Back then, I accepted what I received and didn't know this was something that spoke to my soul. I discovered my love language, physical touch and affirmation unexpectedly. I didn't really believe that a love language existed until now.

Now that I knew what caused me to open up emotionally, mentally, and physically to Love, I didn't know if anything else would.

Carlos would never get this, but between Love and Essex, I was unsure if I could let go of what was to get what I wanted. I didn't like the space I was in, confusion. I needed to decide, and that pretty much had been done with this pregnancy and the dissolution of my and Love's situation, but I wanted what I wanted… I didn't have the patience to hope it ended happily. It didn't.

Love Wins

"All she knew was she missed him,
and nothing made sense
until she could be with him again.

This is what it felt like to fall
and not care where you land."

— N.R. Hart

Essex

Essex was my long-time boyfriend of fifteen years. After three children and years of infidelity resulting in children outside of the relationship, I realized that our relationship was built off sex. After that wore off, we didn't have a very secure foundation to build from. Essex and I simply were not suitable for one another, but we made it work, as dysfunctional as it was. Trauma bonded us, and we just made the best of it. He had proposed to me on several occasions, but I declined each time, so fearful of telling him I didn't want the relationship at all.

"What is it with you?! Why is it that every time I say I want to marry you, you get an attitude?"

My answer was always, "I don't want to talk about it." That would set him off, whew!

"You don't want to talk about it. You never want to talk about it! Nikki, what the hell is wrong with you? I've been asking you to make us permanent for two years now, and I feel like this is going nowhere. Is it because you think I'm still sleeping with Roxanne? Because I told you, we're through."

"Essex, you say that, but you have been with her in the past two years and keep lying about it. Is it that you like me looking crazy out this motherfucker or what?" Yup, I got called crazy for shit that turned out to be true on several occasions. Now he wanted to stand here in my face like his shit didn't stink... nigga, please.

Convinced he had manipulated me once again, he said, "Since you're convinced that I slept with her ass, prove it. If you can't prove it, stop talking about it, damn."

I was not even focused on what the hell it was he was saying after that because I was about to slam him with these receipts, like we were playing Spades, and I just won the book.

I began to read aloud, "'Hey u... kissing emojis... Need you in my mouth.' Any of this ring a bell?" I continue, "'Good morning, luv of my life.' She asked if she's going to see you on June 27th and, oh, what did you say, let me see, 'Yup.' She sent your ass the address, and you said you were in route."

All Essex could do was sit there in silence. He started with, "Babe..."

I stopped him. "I am *not* ya babe, lady, woman, honey... I'm now your ex. You had the audacity to gaslight me over some shit you should've just come clean about, but no, so now we're over."

I kindly told him to get his shit and get the fuck out with his lying, cheating, narcissistic ass.

He wanted to pull our kids into it, and I flipped my shit.

"Was you worried about ya motherfucking kids when you was out here banging these bitches?! No, so don't even purse your lips to even act as if you are so concerned about your family. This relationship has taken its course; it has been a good ride. I never wasted my time, but I learned a lot of lessons. I'm done."

His View

Walking out of the home I had shared for the past five years with Nikki and our children was the hardest thing I'd done. Nikki was right, this relationship had taken its course, and she was done, and I was mostly to blame. I had gathered some of my belongings and told her I'd be back for the rest this weekend. I hopped in my Lincoln Navigator and drove off. I ended up at the Reservoir and walked and cried and cried. At that moment, I realized Nikki always had my back, and I took that for granted.

Roxanne was my weakness; she had been since we were in high school, and she knew that. She told me that was why she acted the way she did toward the others (my other children's mothers, especially Nikki). I knew we would never be together as a couple, but I dabbled every now and then because I knew I could as a man. That had nothing to do with Nikki, but it affected us significantly. Nikki saw it, and I was lying to myself to believe she hadn't. I wanted to call Roxanne and let her know what had happened and stay with her and our son until I got on my feet, but I decided against it because then Nikki would really believe that she and I were still smashing.

I called my mom instead; it was safer that way.

"Mom"

"Hey, son, how you doin'?"

"Well, Nikki kicked me out."

"Again, what is wrong with that girl? She is never satisfied."

"Mom, not this time. I was wrong… She found out Roxanne and I were still messing around."

"Well, son, what did I tell you about messing with her? Ain't nothing gonna come from that and look."

"Mom, stop. That ain't what I need to hear right now. I know I fucked up."

"Give Nikki some time to cool off. She's never mad at you for too long."

"Nah, mom… This is it. It's over."

"Well, where you gonna stay? Cause you can't stay here too long, maybe a couple of days."

"You know what? I'll figure it out. Don't worry about it," I said in anger as I ended the call with my mom.

My mom was the reason I could never commit. She had a way of making me feel invisible and unwanted. My mother's lack of care and concern for me as a boy was why I did what I did; however you look at it. I had four baby moms and six children. My children meant the world to me, but my relationship with their mothers needed much work.

The phone rang.

"Yo bro, I need a place to crash for a minute," I told my brother, Ray.

"Nikki done put ya ass out again, eh?"

"Yeah, for good," I said in embarrassment.

"I got you, bro. Your room's ready. The door's unlocked."

"Thanks, bro."

Ray had been my best friend, more like a brother, since middle school. Whenever I needed a place to stay because I left home or one of these baby moms put me out, Ray was my solid. I remember living with Roxanne, and she found out I was sleeping with Nikki. Man, she burned my shit and sent me on my way. Ray was right there, took me to get some clothes and let me crash with him until I could get back on my feet. I talked Nikki into letting me move in and promised her things were done with Roxanne and me, anything to have a place to stay. What niggas would do when the love wasn't real. This time I'd get my own shit; I couldn't keep going through this.

"I know my worth,
but I didn't know my worth,
and now those lessons
are the path to my life makeover."

— La Dina Strawder

Nicole

I know, call me stupid for listening to other women in my life who were supposed to have some wisdom tell you all the things he did, despite breaking your heart, and that should be my reason to stay and marry. Don't forget those added comments about us having children together. What did that even mean?! Kids received the growth or death of what their parents shared. Why give them an example of bondage and complacency? That was a disservice to them, and I was glad I did what was best for me and not what the asses, I meant masses, wanted me to do.

This relationship came out of insecurities and the need to escape situations both of us were dealing with when we met. My formative years were emotionally and, earlier on, sexually abusive as well as low-key codependent. I felt I needed to be the hero, healer, and savior to everyone at the cost of my own freedom and peace. By eighteen, a sistah was tired. Entering my adult life, I had to learn some hard lessons real quick.

When I met Essex, he was coming out of a relationship with his middle child's mother, Roxanne. She was a bitch then and a bigger bitch now. I rarely call another woman out of her name, out of anger or as a term of endearment, but this chick was. She always wanted to let Essex know that was his child and that he needed to put him first. Her child wasn't Essex's only, but that didn't stop her from trying to ensure her son got what she felt he should have.

Essex, not paying her any attention, so he would say, appeared complacent when I or any of his other baby's moms mentioned it. He would say, "I can't control nobody but me."

His youngest child's mother, Cindy, and I could not stand Roxanne. Although Cindy's son was born while Essex and I were living together, we were determined to be mature adults about the situation, which worked well for our children. I got along well with his oldest children's mother, Trish, but none of us could stand Roxanne. She was one hateful ass bitch toward anyone she remotely thought wanted or who was with Essex. We talked about jumping her, but we're finer women who just decided not to give her the time of day. Her actions made it impossible for us or her son's siblings to bond as we could have and the rest of us wanted to. Essex took a blind eye to all of it.

When I look back, my mother was a catalyst to Essex and me dissolving our relationship; yes, many things added to this, but for the most part, her influence was a deciding factor. She wanted more for her baby girl than she felt Essex could provide. She believed I settled and could do better. I must say, I did settle. I allowed the insecurities of my past to accept someone who cared neither for himself nor me. I could own that part of this mess.

My mother never married my father, and because of that, he made me one of seven or eight siblings. We stopped counting after five. He wasn't the man she wanted him to be to her, although he was an awesome father to my siblings and me.

The hurt she experienced with my father trickled into what she thought I should or should not deal with. She might have been right about what she saw about Essex's and my relationship, but I was not in a place in my life to accept her wisdom; even for my first marriage, she called that too.

I now realize that my trauma prevented me from loving myself first and choosing to be loved the way I required to be loved. After this fiasco with Essex and Love, I chose me.

I didn't just get here. I woke the day after putting Essex out and had to ask myself, "How did you get here, sis?"

Putting up with way more than I needed to from my ex-husband and from Essex, where did I feel I wasn't worth loving? And it hit me; I hadn't loved myself first. How could I expect others to love me truly? That was what I started to do, love myself first and hard.

"No one is responsible for your emotional reactions except you.

Others can say and do anything they like, but what happens inside you is only the result of what you are thinking and feeling."

— Don Miguel Ruiz Jr.
The Mastery of Self

The Straw That Ended It All

Essex

I didn't want it to come to an end with Nikki, but I ended it, and in a bad way. My feelings and I went to social media and "venting." Dumb fucking move on my part, but I was hurt. What else was I supposed to do? Yeah, I could've kept it low-key to spare myself the embarrassment of the whole situation, but what was done was done. Nikki and I were definitely done.

I wrote on Thread It, "This dumb bitch fucked around and got pregnant by another nigga, all while living with me… and now she has the audacity to ask for my support cause dude straight played her… fuck I look like?!"

I was so damned pissed when she told me, thinking, "How could she do this to me?!" In my mind, I was making sure the bills were paid and the kids got what they needed. After all my infidelities, I did everything I knew to make her see I wanted to be with her, and now I knew it was too late. Her heart's coldness had already set in, and I hadn't even noticed it.

In hindsight, I never once stopped to think how she felt when the truth of my infidelity was revealed to her, and I begged and pleaded for her to stay. She even loved my other children like our own. However, at that moment, I felt that the world needed to know what she did to me.

Right after that social media exchange, my mom called me up and said, "People in glass houses shouldn't throw stones. Why the hell are you on social media acting a plumb fool?!"

"She hurt me, so I hurt. . ." I tried to explain, but she cut me off. All I could do was listen.

"Don't give me that! I did not raise you to be out there disrespecting people, especially someone you laid down and made babies with. Be as mad as you want but don't *ever* disrespect a woman like that again. Do I make myself clear? Do I make myself clear?! Boy, don't make me come up there!"

Since I knew my mom would deliver on what she said, I had no choice but to respond, "I hear you loud and clear." I sighed as if it hurt to spit that out.

Mom went on to say how my cousins Chuckie and Brandon called her about my post and wanted to know what was happening with Nikki and me. They screenshotted the post to her, and mom went on and on about how embarrassed she was.

"I know you and Nikki have had y'all moments, but this is overkill to me. Now, take that down."

"Ma, I will," I said; you could hear the irritation in my voice.

I went back to my post and deleted it, but the damage was already done. After my mom called, Chuckie, Brandon and Trish (my baby mom) called me to ask me what the hell my problem was.

Chuckie and Brandon tried to have my back, but they knew all the dirt I had done to Nikki (and the others, my behavior was consistent). However, they needed me to know I had hit an all-time low.

They called me on three-way. "Cuz, what the fuck is you doing?!"

"She deserved that shit." My ego wouldn't let it go.

Brandon was like, "Cuz, c'mon, you done fucked around and had a whole baby on this woman, and now you crushed?! Get over ya self. You put her through a lot, and she forgave ya triflin' ass, and now that you're being served some of your karma, you mad?"

Brandon was my older cousin, one who was like a brother to me; we spent a lot of time at Nana's house growing up, so I respected what he said.

"Cuz, she was dealing with this dude for months while lying in bed with me every night. Yeah, I feel some type of way. I took the post down so you can stop scolding my ass."

Chuckie, part of the cousin-brother club and the oldest of us all and probably the most leveled headed, said, "Stop through tomorrow around 2. We can chop it up a bit with some drinks; I just bought this Patron I want to try. Stacey and the kids will be gone for the day, so you can talk ya shit to us and not Thread It, cool?"

Brandon and I simultaneously said, "Yeah, I'll be over."

Chuckie added with his big brother-like stance, "Bring some wings."

I responded, "I got you, cuz."

Chuckie said, "I'll hit y'all up in the am. Ess, keep ya head up and don't make no more posts. I love ya'll."

Something my grandfather passed on to us as men was that it was not a bad thing to tell another male you love them, especially family and when you meant it.

"Love you too, cuz", we said, hanging up.

I leaned over my bed upside down, looking at the open door to the dark hallway and asked myself, "How did I get here?"

Manly Intervention

Chuckie started our conversation with the same question I asked myself the night before, "Cuz, how did you get here? You ain't never let a woman or human being take you out of character; why her and why now?"

"Cuz, I just snapped. Nikki has never disrespected me the way she did this time and..."

Before I could finish, Chuckie cut me off.

"So you expected her to continue being hella gracious and longsuffering with your shit, but she step out one time, and you crying like a little bitch? When they said men can't take a woman cheating, you just proved them absolutely right."

"Look, cuz. I didn't come over here to be bashed for some shit I know I was wrong for," I said defensively.

"My bad, cuz, but Granddad is rolling over in his grave knowing how you're showing up for yourself right now, bitch move."

This was his way of apologizing, but he was right. Grandad would've cussed me out for not handling myself with more self-control. That was what men did, control themselves in every situation.

"I love her!" I blurted out.

Chuckie and Brandon both looked at me with their eyes wide open 'cause none of us had ever made a declaration as serious as this. We were men, but we never let the L-word touch our lips with any woman, especially when we were out here running up in any woman we could finesse.

"Yo!" They outright laughed, just chuckled when they saw I was serious.

I loved Nikki. She was there for me through many of my growing pains, and I just thought she would always be there whether I grew up or not; I took her for granted, and now I was paying for it. Lesson learned.

We continued to drink, chop it up, and watched a replay of the Steelers' game to pass the time and keep my mind off the biggest mistake of my life.

Nikki

This dude had the nerve to go on Thread It and try to expose me. I wouldn't have known unless some of our mutual "friends" tagged me in his post.

I replied, "Dude, we currently reside in the same house, so for you to get on here acting funny is dumb as hell. Furthermore, you act as if you didn't see this coming with your neglectful, cheating, lying ASS."

He went on to tell the internet how I cheated and got pregnant by another dude. So now I was ready to tell all, but Camille and a couple of my cousins texted me and told me to chill. They knew I would have lit his ass up on there. I was about to drag his ass for real, for real. I did a little bit. This nigga gone say, "You did me dirty, and you're about to lose it all."

"You done lost everything doing me dirty, even ya got damn hairline, tf!" I wrote in sweet retaliation. I blocked him after that. He just showed how motherfucking toxic he was and why I chose to leave.

My cousins Presh and Lossa facetimed me to calm me down 'cause they knew how I got down.

"Cuz, woosah," they said. "I'm so glad he deleted that post 'cause you was about to hand him his whole entire ass."

Lossa laughed, saying, "If you need a recap, I screenshotted that shit! She went in on him!"

"I wouldn't have did all that had he not posted that. I ain't never went to social media all the times he did me dirty, that I didn't deserve."

Here came Presh (the oldest cousin and more spiritual than me), "Cuz, you got to bless and not curse."

"Cuz, be glad I didn't tell his ass to go to Hell. That would be a curse. I stated facts. His receding ass hairline is a fact and not a curse; someone beat me to it."

Lossa, being no help, laughed, "Yooo, I'm in tears! Cuz, stop it!"

Presh said, "Cuz, come on, you could have handled yourself better than that."

Lossa, after she stopped laughing, agreed, "Yeah, cuz, you could have. I understand why, but you're more refined than that."

"Ya'll right, but right now, I reacted how I reacted because he wasn't and isn't going to keep making me out to be the bad guy. He has done more dirt in this relationship that I've dealt with as a dumb-dumb. So now, I'm done, and he can kiss my pregnant ass."

"Yeah! So, when was you gonna tell us you were knocked the hell up, cousin?!" Lossa asked.

"See, what had happened was…" I explained Love's and my relationship all the way up to now. Surprisingly, my cousins, as much as we loved each other, would trash and criticize one another for our poor choices just as quickly. They showed me grace this time.

Expressing how they would be there for me, they started planning my shower as we talked.

Presh said, "I'm here to support you, cuz. Love will come around. Just be ready to forgive and move on whether y'all are together or not 'cause now you all have a child to love, support and care for."

Here came Lossa on her shit, "Well, this is your exit to leave Essex's raggedy ass... You know I never cared for him, treating you like that. You betta than me 'cause I would've cut that street meat and went on my way."

"Street meat, cuz, you crazy!"

All you heard was laughter.

"Love y'all, but I gotta go," Presh said. "Talk to y'all later."

Amends

It took well into my third trimester for Essex to come around and support me as I supported him with his children. I deserved that much. Essex could be a good man when he wanted to, but those other times, the damn Gemini was running rampant, and that was the part of him I wanted to cap… pew, pew nigga. We cool now y'all.

He was a tremendous help during my pregnancy, as well as our children and my family; even Trish was helpful. Essex escorted me to every prenatal appointment. Since we had three of our own, we didn't need Lamaze classes. Our children were at an age where they could comprehend what was going on and offered support and did more chores than asked to do to keep my pressure down. They were excited about a younger sibling. My mom, dad, and other relatives supported me as well. My mom and dad were thankful to Essex for supporting me at such a critical time.

I was thankful. I had my own little tribe to love on me and make this pregnancy so amazing. Trish happened to be a doula, so she walked me through my whole pregnancy. When I would bawl my eyes out about Love not being active, she gave me assignments to reduce my stress and focus on having a healthy baby. Although I realized Love was not present to share this experience with me, love was present in and around me. I accepted it wholeheartedly.

My tribe threw me the most beautiful baby shower I ever had. To walk into so many hues of pink, tiaras, and melanin princesses was a sight to see. My little princess would not have to want for anything. Everyone wanted to know what I'd name her, but I decided not to reveal this information until she was born.

That day was June 8th, and the most chocolate 7lb 5oz baby was born.

She looked like Love. I teared up when they laid her my breasts. Life changed for me as a woman and a mom in the past year, and that was a great thing. As I looked at this beautiful being God had given me, I knew I had been saved from a lot of hurt and pain through this love.

Love Wins

"One day love will come in the form of
someone who wants to
give more than take,
and you will know why
LOVE is rare."

— Mark Anthony (FB)

Happy Endings

"What if it does work out exactly how you imagined it or greater. Entertain that thought."

— Author Unknown

Do happy endings exist? We watch so many animated movies that a few of us still want to believe that one day we will meet our princess or that our prince will find us. I remember hoping things would work out was a part of my logic growing up in a dysfunctional home. "Something has to be better than what I have gone through," I would think.

I never wanted that for my children and tried hard to prevent being the cause of their "issues." I found history repeating itself and needed to get out of the dysfunction with Essex because, at the end of the day, my hope would be for the world to see the real love between my man and me. I wanted to be the #relationshipgoals everyone aspired to have. I realized I needed to work on myself before I could welcome love when he came. Self-work, self-development, whatever you wanted to call it, was necessary for growth and for those blessings to be received on your end; begin where it all started.

I read a lot. I looked up words and came across the definition of what I had been through in my life. It was called adversity: difficulties, misfortune, hardship, trouble, bad luck. I always questioned God about my experiences because none of them made me have faith in a loving creator. I was beginning to believe "this is how things will always be" until I met Love. I hurt every time I remembered how we ended; the consolation to that relationship was that he was a man of his word, for the most part. That was the love I imagined God was like, and I wanted more of it, but I feared it was too late. The only positive thing I could reflect on was the beautiful child he had given me. The child he didn't even know he had.

"We can't live in freedom if we constantly allow our toxic thoughts to monopolize our thinking," my life coach, Tirzha, told me as we were in one of our sessions.

'Cause I get a little dense, I needed her to break her wise words down for me.

"For example," she said. "If *you* continually tell yourself that things aren't going to get better, you eventually *believe* and *poison* your own mind and therefore get stuck in that negative mindset. If *you* speak life into your situation, it can change in a positive direction."

That was the day I opted to choose positivity, contentment, happiness.

"If I want a happy ending, damn it," I thought. "I have to stop thinking it can't happen to or for me."

This was pivotal in dealing with the break-up with Essex, which wasn't easy after so many years together. I just didn't want to become complacent in familiar situations. With this, I had to accept the part I played in my own unnecessary misery and causing someone else pain. I should have walked away sooner, but fear gripped me something bad. I had to release my hand from what was keeping me back from life, from living, from my own growth.

I was determined to experience my latter being greater, and it took courage despite the reality that brought it about. I got real brand new; the change was really noticeable. I recalled Camille commenting on it when I facetimed her to tell her the news about being pregnant.

Camille talked about my glow, "Sis, who you got new because that glow you got is whoa?"

"I don't have a man in my life right now, but this baby I'm carrying may be doing it," I responded.

"Wait, what?! Yo ass is pregnant and ain't tell nobody?! I'm so confused," she said with a sigh. "Why you leave Essex if you're pregnant?"

"Sis, I hope you're sitting down. I have something to tell you."

"I am now! Hold on while I pull this Henny out 'cause, sis, you got a bitch rattled like a motherfucker," she laughingly sighed. "OK, first shot taken; now, what you mean you're pregnant?!"

"I'm pregnant, three and a half months to be exact. It's not Essex's, and I didn't see a reason to stay together and fake like it was."

"Sis! What the fuck?!" She shook her head in disbelief at the news. "Are you fucking serious right now?!"

"Yes, sis, he and I both knew it would come to this."

"But damn, pregnant?! It's gonna take me a moment to get past that part. Well, if Essex ain't the daddy, who is?" she asked.

"Sis, you ain't neva gonna believe whose it is." I gave her that sheepish smile and shook my head.

She started to name people, "Carlos? James? Corey? Marques? Keith? Naw, that nigga was fugly… I hope it ain't Keith's; it ain't Keith, is it?" she asked nervously.

"Bitch... No, it ain't no Keith's!" I exclaimed.

With a sigh of relief, she said, "Whoa, cause that baby would be gorillafied ugly."

We both started falling out laughing.

"Okay, okay, so you know when I told you I saw Love again?" I asked, jogging her memory.

"I know you fucking lying," she answered in disbelief. "Love done got you knocked up and ain't hit you up since?" she said, pissed.

"Naw, sis, it wasn't like that," I tried calming her down to explain what really went down.

"Do tell! A sistah needs to know."

I explained how Love and I reconnected randomly after years of not seeing one another. I repeated his cheesy ass line, "God put us together."

She laughingly said, "You know that nigga always had a corny ass pickup line, but it must not have been that corny." She looked down at my stomach.

"Bitch, shut up!" I laughed. "Anyway, both of us were in relationships, but the attraction we had was still there after all those years. You already know what I was going through with Essex, so we hooked up, and when I told him I needed to walk away from this to focus on my business with Essex, he fell all the way off, and then I found out I was pregnant. Don't be mad at Love. Besides, no one knows we were messing around anyway."

"Sis, you've got to try to tell him."

"Naw, if he wanted to be bothered with me like he said, he'd be around or would have contacted me. I learned after Essex not to chase no man. If a man wants you, it will be obviously clear and consistent."

"Yeah," Camille agreed. "We ain't gon' be no man's chicken head, eating up the molded crumbs he throws at us 'cause we ain't the only one he is throwing them to. Catch that." Camille encouraged, "At least try to reach out."

"I have no desire to contact Love." I expressed.

Maybe it was emotions from this pregnancy. Maybe my happy ending was this baby, and I had to be okay with that.

Love Wins

"I fell in love with you.
I don't know how;
I don't know why.
I just did."

— Author Unknown

Five Years Later

I was walking out of the store at a small shopping plaza near the house when I heard someone call my name. I was concerned because I'd been in North Carolina for two years since I left Pittsburgh. I thought, "Who the hell is calling my name?"

Even Zuri Issa looked confused.

"Mommy." She pointed to a man walking towards us. "That man is calling you."

I turned, and to my surprise, it was Love. Butterflies danced in my stomach, but the disappointment he left me with overshadowed all that. He could tell by the look on my face that he had some explaining to do. He must come up with a big excuse for why he ghosted me after I decided not to be with him. He wouldn't answer my calls since then. He didn't even know we had a daughter.

Love leaned in for a hug, and I stiffened.

"Long time no see," he said as he looked down at Zuri Issa. "Hey, pretty girl."

Her almond-shaped chestnut eyes stared intently at him. I didn't know if she was amazed at his height or if she was trying to protect me from him.

She looked up and introduced herself, "Hi, I'm Zuri. Nice to meet you."

My baby was so kind and intelligent for an almost five-year-old.

I looked confused, and he was looking just as confused.

"Why are you acting so standoffish?" he asked.

"I haven't seen or spoken to you in about five years, so why are you acting like we were just casual?" I asked.

Love was more confused. "Nikki, what are you talking about?"

"You ghosted my a—" I stopped myself. I tried not to use bad language around Zuri. "You ghosted me. You didn't answer any of my calls, so sorry, not sorry, if I seem a bit standoffish."

Love grinned, but I saw nothing funny. I thought to myself, "Here he go, trying to reel me in. He still had his way of making me love him, even when I wanted to hate him."

"Babe, it wasn't even like that."

"Then what was it?" I asked.

"I ended up changing my number because of some crazy chick I was dealing with. I shut down my social media accounts because she was crazy as fuck. I had to get a PFA and everything."

I just looked at him.

"Babe," he continued. "I'm sorry you felt that way. I was never trying to play you. I told you that from day one. I didn't want to pull you into my bull. Besides, you said you were cutting me for old dude, and I told you I wasn't going to bring no drama into what we had going on."

"You're right," was all I could say. I felt myself breaking.

Love gave me a tight but gentle hug, and I melted. It sent me back to the times we had [been] together where all the BS we faced didn't matter.

"You could've said something," I insisted.

"You're right, babe, but here we are now. All my bullshit is done. I left everything back in Pittsburgh. I'm here now, so?" He looked at me as if to say, "Can we start over?"

Curious, I asked, "So, what are you doing in North Carolina?"

"After all that drama and remembering you saying that North Carolina had so much to offer, I decided to move here to get a fresh start," he said.

"How long have you been down here?" I asked.

"About six months now," he said. "I applied for some contracting jobs. That's the plus for working for myself. I can kind of move around."

He looked down at Zuri and admired her quietness as we talked. "Do you mind if I give her some candy?" He took some candy out of his pocket. "She has been so quiet and patient with us catching up."

"I can't tell her father what he can and cannot give her."

His eyes lit up in amazement. "You fucking lying?! We have a daughter?!" Love asked, bewildered.

"No, ninja, we have a parakeet. Yes, we have a daughter!" I knelt to get to eye level with Zuri. "Zuri, you know how you always ask me where your dad is, baby?" I asked.

"Yes, Mommy, and you say when you pray, God will let me meet him."

"Yes, baby, and today God is answering your prayers."

Her little face said she didn't understand quite what I was telling her, but she knew God answered prayers.

"Zuri," I said. "I want you to meet your father, DeVaughn Lovely."

Love swooped her up as if she had been in his life this whole time, and Zuri didn't mind it one bit.

"DeVaughn, meet your daughter, Zuri Issa Lovely."

They didn't miss a beat.

I looked at them and teased, "Is that a tear I see, my G?"

"Shut up, man," Love laughed. "Let me have my moment with my baby girl."

I smiled and let him have his moment.

After our meet and greet, Love and I exchanged numbers. I told him, "You make the move this time. I'll wait."

"I most definitely will, I most definitely will," he said without hesitation.

Always a man of his word, Love called while I was helping Zuri strap herself in her car seat. Like her mother, she liked to be independent. I gave the phone to her, and she talked to him as if he had always been there.

I let them talk until she said, "Mommy, my daddy wants to talk to you."

I reach behind my seat to grab the phone from her hand.

Zuri, with her brightness, suggested, "Mommy, why don't you just use the car Bluetooth?"

Shaking my head and smiling, I thought, "This girl never ceases to amaze me."

I used my lovebug's suggestion and connected the Bluetooth to the car.

"You're on speaker phone," I emphasized to Love. "Zuri can hear you."

"Thanks for the heads up. I just want to make plans to take you beautiful ladies out on a date if you are up to it."

"Yes." Zuri danced in her car seat. "Yes!"

I turned around to look at her.

"Please, Mommy?" Zuri begged. "Please, please, please?!"

"Whatever you want, baby girl… We can go on a date."

Love and I planned to take Zuri out to this trampoline park not too far from either of us that following weekend.

"Well, it's set. I will pick you ladies up at 11 a.m. on Saturday."

We heard the excitement in Zuri's voice when she said, "Bye, Daddy!"

"Bye, baby girl. Daddy loves you."

We ended the call, and Zuri asked.

"Mommy, is that really my daddy?"

"Yes, Zuri. What made you ask that?"

"I didn't think God would answer my prayers, and I wanted to make sure."

All I could do was smile at her innocence and truthful conversation. I thought, "If only we could stay like this with one another as adults and with God."

I told Zuri our favorite saying, "He may not come when you want Him, but He comes right on time."

She finished the sentence with me.

"That's right, baby girl, God comes *right* on time!"

"Thank you, Father," I silently prayed.

That evening, I was talking to my oldest son, Emmanuel, affectionately known as Manny. Zuri loved talking to her siblings, and I thought they got a kick out of talking to her.

Zuri said, "Manny, guess what?"

I could hear Manny through the phone saying, "What?"

"I met my dad today!"

You know kids, they tell *all* the business.

Manny, excited for his sister, said, "You did?! Tell me all about it."

And she did… for a good twenty-five minutes. She gave him the deets and told him how he looked to her from her tiny little world.

"He was a giant," she told Manny.

When she was done giving her events for the day and handed me the phone, I braced myself because I knew Manny. He had as many questions as his sister.

"Mom, you didn't tell me Zuri's dad was in North Carolina."

"Manny, I didn't know he moved down here until I saw him today."

"Aren't you glad, though? You've wanted to tell him about Zuri for a long time now."

Manny always had a way of seeing the glass of life as half full.

"I'm happy for you, for Zuri. I prayed for this day for you both."

"I love you, son."

I was tearing up at the realization that my prayers from almost five years ago were being answered.

"I am so thankful. You are the best son and brother Zuri and I could have"

I wondered, "What will come of all of this?" I'd learned to be present and live in the moment and try not to control the outcome. I prayed and did my part, and that was what I would do.

Zuri woke up so early Saturday morning because she knew what today meant. She would see her daddy, like she hadn't seen him the other day, but I wouldn't kill her vibe. I knew this was all new for her; hell, it was new for me.

She ran to the door when she heard a knock.

She screamed, "Mommy, Mommy, my Daddy's here!"

I chuckled at her excitement. "Ask who it is, and if he says 'Daddy.'" I was sitting on the loveseat in the den, putting on my yellow Sketchers. "Open the door for him, okay?"

When Love entered the sitting room, he tried cracking on me about my Sketchers, but all I could say was, "Oh, you'll see."

Zuri and Love bonded so quickly that it amazed me to tears. It reminded me of the bond I had with my dad at her age.

"I hope this never changes for them," I thought.

Zuri surely put his energy to the test! She wanted him to jump at every station, and he, like a show-off, did. He needed a nap after we left the jump park, but I made him drive us home.

"Damn, it's been a long time since I ran after a kid, and she got mad energy. How did you do this shit for four years?! I don't think I was this tired raising my older kids."

"I tried to tell you." All I could do was shake my head and laugh at him. "But what do I know? You should have known what you were getting into when you have an almost five-year-old."

"These new-age kids are built differently. Their turn-up is on 1000 from jump." He sighed. "I am going to pay for this tomorrow."

"Should have worn your Sketchers," I teased. "These are the best shoes for when I'll be on my feet all day with our little lady."

I patted his leg to offer some sympathy for his tiredness.

"Real Love" started playing as Love turned onto the main road in his Black Cadillac Escalade. We looked at each other and bust out laughing.

"This is a sign," he said.

"Pump your brakes, "I told him. "Let's get you used to being a father to our princess."

I looked back and patted Zuri's leg. As always, he paid me no mind, and as I looked into his eyes, I sensed he strongly believed this was a sign. I didn't even argue. I sat back, rested my head on the headrest and sang along with Mary like I was her backup singer.

"Lord knows I need a real love," I thought.

Journal Entry

Love, for many of us, has not been patient nor kind. It has been boastful, unforgiving, and toxic, as well as cyclical. All lessons are learned when you don't want to repeat the cycle of toxic relationships. We run from relationship to relationship, looking for someone to love us, not realizing the real one to love is the person we see in the mirror every single day. We accept abuse, infidelity, and degradation at the cost of wanting what we believe is real love. Let these situations be a catalyst to get you to see that you are worthy of love, real love.

Love keeps us accountable but will not seek satisfaction in wanting you to "learn your lesson the hard way." That is a slave mentality. Slaves received harsh punishment to obey slave owners who would come and rape their women and be told by their punishers how much they appreciated and loved them.

You are part of a Kingdom that cannot be torn down or destroyed. First, you must love yourself. Work on yourself, whether it be attending a worship service, therapy, coaching. People will love you how you love yourself. Maybe, just maybe, that one you shared a mutual love with will return to love you better than they did initially. Until then, love God, love yourself, love others… in that order (in my Mama Dee voice).

ACKNOWLEDGMENTS

Artist-Ikenna N. Chineme, thank you for allowing me to showcase your art with this cover.

Penda L. James, my Scribe Coach, thank you for your continued support and mentorship through this project.

Soleil Meade, thank you for bringing my vision to life!

RESOURCES

Love Wins

If you need support, here are a few resources to consider:

- National Domestic Violence Hotline: 800-799-7233
- SAMHSA's National Helpline: 1-800-662-4357
- March of Dimes: 1-888-663-4637 (888-MODIMES)

DISCUSSION QUESTIONS

Love Wins

Love Wins: Nikki's Tale touches some delicate subjects. This book will help you reminisce about your childhood years as well as provide insight on how to navigate this thing called life. The following questions are conversation starters that will help you, or your group reflect and gather gems about love, dreaming bigger, and redefining your relationships.

1. What was high school like for you? (What music did you listen to and what was your favorite outfit?)

2. Did you attend your prom? If you didn't do you wish you had?

3. Did you have a best friend in high school? How does Nikki and Camille's relationship align with or differ from what you and your best friend had?

4. Nikki indicates a trauma of being molested by a family member. Her mom swept it under the rug and the only person she felt would protect her was her cousin, Jason. Do you believe there a correlation between Nikki feeling protected and heard as it pertains to her interaction with the opposite sex. How do you think her father would have reacted?

5. Have you ever experienced trauma in your life, if so, were their people you could confide in? What was their reaction and how did it make you feel?

6. Camille experienced intimate partner violence (IPV) while in college. If you have experienced IPV, what was the reaction of people in your life when you told them what was happening? What was your reaction when someone told you they were experiencing IPV?

7. When Camille told Nikki of her breast cancer diagnosis how did she respond? Knowing that they were able to discuss it, do you feel that Nikki was justified in her response? How would you have responded?

8. What do you think is the reason Nikki never gave Love a chance as teenagers besides his upbringing? Have you had that a mutual interest in someone but felt they were off limits? Why?

9. Do you feel as if Nikki and Love's situationship could have been handled differently? In what way?

10. In the day of social media a lot of fights go on between people (i.e., friends, lovers, family). What was your take on Essex and Nikki's social media exchange?

11. In the case of Nikki, Zuri, and Love do you feel as if love wins for them? What does it look like for love to win for you?

12. What has always been your dream? How can you dream bigger? Do you feel you have attained it? If not, what can you start today to make it happen?

13. In the African- American culture, many, men are taught not to show emotion, communicate how they feel, or even say "I love you" to one another. What impression did Essex and his cousins' interaction leave on you? Do men of color have supports like this? Do you believe it is hard for men to say I love you to other men (relatives and children)? Discuss your perspective.

14. Essex faults his relationship with his mother as to the reason his relationships with his children's mothers were rocky. What would be your perspective of the situation?

15. Men, discuss the men in your life that keep you accountable like Chuckie and Brandon. How have men like this impacted your growth as a man?

16. Do you agree that men handle infidelity differently than women? Why?

17. African-American women have the highest rates of low birth weight babies and trauma during pregnancy and labor & delivery. How can parents reduce stress in a women's life during pregnancy?

I'm looking forward to connecting with you. Follow me on social media for updates on how you can meet me at an event near you!

IG: @Author_LaDina

Author LaDina

AuthorLaDina@gmail.com

LIFE HAS ITS STRUGGLES BUT WE ARE NOT ALONE IN IT
LIFE HAS ITS STRUGGLES BUT WE ARE NOT ALONE IN IT
LIFE HAS ITS STRUGGLES BUT WE ARE NOT ALONE IN IT
LIFE HAS ITS STRUGGLES BUT WE ARE NOT ALONE IN IT
LIFE HAS ITS STRUGGLES BUT WE ARE NOT ALONE IN IT
LIFE HAS ITS STRUGGLES BUT WE ARE NOT ALONE IN IT
LIFE HAS ITS STRUGGLES BUT WE ARE NOT ALONE IN IT
LIFE HAS ITS STRUGGLES BUT WE ARE NOT ALONE IN IT

Love Wins

www.ingramcontent.com/pod-product-compliance
Lightning Source LLC
LaVergne TN
LVHW012331100826
845148LV00017B/2110

* 9 7 9 8 2 1 8 1 9 4 4 5 1 *